An Accidental Marriage

An Accidental Marriage

DEBORAH M. HATHAWAY

Books by Deborah M. Hathaway

A Cornish Romance (Regencies)

On the Shores of Tregalwen, a Prequel Novella

Behind the Light of Golowduyn, Book One

For the Lady of Lowena, Book Two

Near the Ruins of Penharrow, Book Three

In the Waves of Tristwick, Book Four

From the Fields of Porthlenn, Book Five

Men of the Isles (RomCom)

Winning Winnie's Hand, Book One

Driving Maisie Crazy, Book Two

Ruling out Robyn, Book Three

Multi-Author Series (Regencies)

The Cottage by Coniston

Carving for Miss Coventry

To Know Miss May

Love Is for the Birds

Multi-Author Series (RomCom)

Christmas Baggage

Multi-Author Series (Christmas Regencies)

Nine Ladies Dancing

On the Second Day of Christmas

To Erin,

*For listening, helping, teaching,
and believing in me.*

Prologue

English Channel, December 1810

English Channel, December 1810. The sea punished *The Siren* with battering waves, angrily swiping its paws against the bulwark again and again in a frenzied attempt to capsize the twenty-passenger packet ship.

Charles Shepherd and his twin, Tristan, had been waiting out the storm in their own private cabin, speaking of distracting stories from their childhood before they'd been pulled into another friend's cabin. Now, the seven childhood schoolmates squished together in the same room.

"If we die tonight, at least we die together," Thomas had said.

With Sweden declaring war on England a few weeks before, they'd chosen to cut their Grand Tour short, though traveling across the treacherous sea from Europe to England was proving menacing enough in its own right.

The seven of them had met at Winchester when they were young. They'd managed to maintain their friendships—and their lives—until now, though many of them now believed that death was imminent.

Hence the wager Thomas had concocted. The wager they were now all agreeing to, with Charles's turn swiftly approaching.

"If I live, I swear I'll do my duty by Miss Delafield!" Rowan Ashworth shouted in the bunk nearby.

"You'll never marry her!" Leonard returned in the bunk next to him.

Charles and Tristan laughed where they sat near the door of the cabin, both of them seated on stools that had been nailed to the floor. Though they fiercely clung to the sides, occasionally one of them would fly off their perch and knock the other down. Bruises and sore bones accompanied their unhinged laughter—laughter induced from stress, but laughter, nonetheless.

More words were spoken nearby, but Charles couldn't hear over the sound of the raging sea and groaning bulwark.

He wasn't particularly concerned about death *or* the wager. One hundred pounds to be paid to each individual by the friend who was last to marry would hardly put a dent in his pocket case. At any rate, he had no intention of marrying until he knew it was right—with a woman who was right for him. Specifically a woman whom he would spend the rest of his days with, seeking one adventure after another.

"But can you beat the rest of us to the altar?" Tristan called out in response to more words Charles hadn't heard.

Further chuckling sounded.

From his viewpoint, Charles could see each of his friends. Andrew Langford settled the swinging lantern just above another bunk as Ambrose Hartley—who they affectionately called Rosie—wiped the sweat that matted his hair against his brow.

Thomas Denby and Leonard Stanton—who had a fierce scowl on his brow—sat nearby with folded arms and wary glances cast to the walls, as if they feared the water rushing in through the slabs of wood.

They weren't wrong to worry. But Charles had always found life to be far more exciting when not filled with trepidation.

Tristan nudged him with his boot, tossing his head to the others. Charles's turn had come. He drew a deep breath, shouting, "I, Charles Shepherd, swear to fulfill the wager!"

Tristan followed shortly after, then the two gave each other a look. No one spoke for a moment, allowing another roaring thunder to have its time in the spotlight.

"Shouldn't be too difficult to find a wife," Tristan said, his voice only reaching Charles's ear, "what with Mother's plans to marry us off the minute we return home."

"Precisely why I intend *not* to return home," Charles countered.

"You mean to die out here?" Tristan returned with a sardonic lift of his brow.

"Death *would* be a thrilling adventure, but not exactly what I meant. I merely have other plans to keep me from returning to Grendale Manor for the foreseeable future."

"Very wise!" Tristan shouted over another crack of thunder and resulting rush of waves.

More promises were set forth, and Charles clung harder to his stool. They would make it alive out of this storm. He would *will* it if he had to.

He hadn't spent years at Winchester then Cambridge to end his freedom now at sea. He had his whole life ahead of him, and nothing was going to stop his next adventure from coming.

So let the ship capsize. Let the sea try to swallow him whole. Heavens, let *Mother* try to pressure him into a marriage.

He was ready to combat it all.

Chapter One

Surrey, *March 1816*

Charles Shepherd was not known for being anxious. He rarely felt uneasy and *never* entertained worrisome thoughts. He was as calm as the sea on a cool day and as carefree as a new leaf basking in the balminess of a spring sunshine.

But this morning, as he rode across the green fields of Dorking, he could not help the impending dread slithering toward him.

The dark clouds cloaking Surrey did not help his unease, nor did his black gelding stamping the ground nervously and snorting out great puffs of white air in the cold.

But something else was troubling him even more, and that would not be settled until he faced it head on.

Westburn House appeared within his view low in the fields, a round drive leading to a simple brown exterior with a dozen windows divided between two floors.

He'd seen the house countless times before, having grown up only a few miles away, though he hadn't seen *any* of Dorking for the last few months, due to his extended stay with Rowan at Ashworth Hall for Christmas and Ambrose and Tristan in London for the following winter months.

Because of his absence, he had yet to meet Westburn's new tenants, the Oakleys. They'd taken possession of the estate only the year before. This was why he had come—to pay his respects to Mr. and Mrs. Oakley.

And of course there was the somewhat microscopic matter of having agreed to meet *Miss* Oakley, the Oakleys' *"very amiable and very single daughter."*

Charles grimaced. Mother and Father had spent the better part of the last year attempting to pull Charles toward Miss Oakley and all of her *"many accomplishments."*

Charles had managed to finagle his way out of meeting the woman for months now, but he'd promised to return home some-day, and unfortunately, "someday" was now.

Only the promise of a ride across the countryside had pulled him toward Surrey this morning—and the guarantee that Mother would stop pushing him toward Miss Oakley if he agreed to meet her. So he had.

After his visit with the Oakleys—which, heaven willing, would only take a quarter of an hour—Charles would be ready for his trip to Leicestershire with Tristan where they would enjoy a well-deserved holiday, fishing, hunting, and enjoying the sunshine.

What a delight that sounded. Far more than meeting with a woman he had less interest in than a cold.

He entered the grounds of the Oakleys' estate, the gentle thudding of his horse's hooves shifting from grass to crunching gravel. With each new step, he drew closer to fulfilling his duty of contributing to Mother's happiness.

Her favorite pastime was setting her sons up with one woman after another, convinced that each new female would be the answer to her sons' joyous futures. Tristan had thus far managed to evade the worst of her attempts thanks to Charles. Charles was the oldest—by three minutes and thirteen seconds—so he was happy to help his brother, even if he had to deal with the brunt of Mother's meddling matchmaking.

First it had been Miss Beaumont with her five-thousand-pound dowry. Then there had been the heiress Miss Fitzroy, and the year after that, Miss Grant, with her red hair that would have made *"the loveliest of babies."* Now, it was Miss Oakley and her unmatched accomplishments.

Miss Oakley is too serene for your brother. You, Charles, are in need of a gentle touch, and she is sure to give it, as she is the most charming woman. You will not, I am certain, find her equal in beauty and goodness in all of England. I am convinced, as is your father, that you two would make a most happy match.

Miss Oakley has also expressed interest in an arranged marriage, as she is, perhaps, a mere degree older than your average female—I believe quite near your age. I know how you feel about such arrangements, but has your opinion, perhaps, changed? How you would make my maternal heart sing if it has!

There was always more to her letters, but Charles's interest typically drifted off after a couple paragraphs. Still, knowing Mother and her crafty ways, this Miss Oakley could very well be nearing fifty.

He shifted uncomfortably in his saddle, the leather creaking with his movements. His horse snorted in protest, feeling his master's discomfort. Charles gave the gelding a settling pat on his black neck.

The very idea of an arranged marriage was preposterous. Just because his parents had agreed to one that had miraculously proven happy did not mean Charles wanted to take that risk himself. He wanted to marry for love—he wanted a happy life, a happy home, a happy future with the woman *he* chose.

He was five and twenty this year, which only amplified Mother's attempts, but he was in no rush to marry. Not even Thomas

Denby's ridiculous wager six years earlier could convince him to change his opinion. Or the fact that Andrew Langford had been added to the growing list of men becoming leg shackled. Charles enjoyed his adventures with his friends and Tristan too greatly to give them up for a life as a husband and father just yet.

He'd expressed such for years, but Mother would not relent. Especially with Miss Oakley. Charles had to admit, though he loved his parents and knew they meant well, the constant pressuring had gotten to him.

He often ignored her letters, but after the eighth one delivered this year alone—and more than two dozen about Miss Oakley since the beginning of *last* year—he had finally responded in the only way he knew how.

With delightful satire.

Very well, you've convinced me. Arrange the marriage. Set the date. Order the flowers. Send out the invitations. Read the banns. Purchase a ring for her, will you?

But one simple request: might I meet my future wife first?

He'd ended his correspondence with the date he'd planned to return to Dorking, but Mother didn't respond for nearly a fortnight. She was obviously unamused by his sarcasm and had chosen to ignore it. She'd merely told him she'd set the date and location for their meeting, that she and Father would be there to alleviate any discomfort, and then ended with two simple statements.

Thank you for agreeing to this, son. I know you will love her.

He had very little hope that he would. Between Thomas's letter reinstating their boyhood wager and Mother's meddling, it felt as if all of England was pressing him toward bliss-less matrimony.

But all of that was no matter. He didn't need to love Miss Oakley. Not for a minimal, quarter-of-an-hour visit.

He reached the front doors of Westburn where he dismounted, and a groom took the reins from his hands. Charles peered up at the house, then straightened his jacket with a deep breath.

Fifteen minutes. A simple introduction, pleasantries exchanged, then he would be free.

Time to get this over with.

Marie Oakley peered out of the window at the gravel drive, her eyes fixed on the gentleman who stood before Westburn's doors.

Mr. Charles Shepherd.

She couldn't see much of him from her viewpoint, but he was tall and had a thick head of hair that he was currently running his fingers through. Was he as handsome as Mrs. Shepherd claimed? Mothers weren't particularly trustworthy when it came to being impartial to their sons.

He shook his hands out at the side of him, then walked toward the front door and out of sight.

"He has arrived," Marie said simply, moving away from the window to rejoin Mother, Father, and Mr. and Mrs. Shepherd by the hearth.

They watched her with smiles and excitement, but Marie kept her eyes trained on the crackling fire.

If she made eye contact with Mother, Marie might voice just how very much she didn't wish to go through with this. If she made eye contact with Father, she might just beg him to reconsider her age of eight and twenty being so very *"on the shelf."* And if she made eye contact with the Shepherds, she'd be filled with an all-encompassing guilt for contemplating reneging on her decision to finally agree to the arrangement.

It was too late to change her mind now. She kept her gaze averted until footsteps sounded just outside the door, signaling the arrival of the much-awaited gentleman.

Only then did Marie face forward with a deep breath.

It was time.

Time to meet her betrothed and to *marry* her betrothed.

Chapter Two

"Mr. Charles Shepherd."

The butler announced his name, and Charles rounded the corner, entering the Oakleys' parlor and coming face-to-face with a room full of expectant eyes.

He bowed, then took in the sight before him. His first impression was that of the space being stiff and rigid, not only in appearance, but in atmosphere, as well. The air was chilled despite the fire, and the color of the walls a drab brown—made even more so due to gray light filtering in through the window at the back of the room.

The people were no more exuberant.

Charles took a few steps within the room, pulling on a pleasant expression as he eyed his parents exactly where they said they'd be. Mother's smile was tight, Father's nearly non-existent.

Obviously, they wanted this meeting to go well. Charles would be the perfect gentleman they expected, but he already knew this meeting was not going to result in love-at-first-sight—as his parents so clearly desired.

Still, he had to admit he was curious to see Miss Oakley, if only to celebrate his accuracy in predicting her extended age.

When he finally turned to face her, he found her entirely hidden behind the stiff and imposing figure of her father.

Before anything was said, Mother rushed toward Charles, delivering a gentle embrace. "My darling son. How pleased I am to see you." Then she whispered into his ear, "You have made my heart...so happy."

Her voice broke between her words, and when she pulled back, tears shone in her eyes.

Crying? That was a bit dramatic, considering all he'd agreed to do was meet the woman.

"Anything for you, Mother."

She gave a little laugh. "Your recurrent protesting would say otherwise."

"Son," Father greeted next with a clasp on his shoulder, "happy to see you've safely arrived."

"As am I, Father."

Charles glanced once again to the Oakleys. Miss Oakley was still slightly hidden, only her black hair visible and the top of one arched brow. Mrs. Oakley stood at the side of her daughter, short, thin, and staring with a slightly absent-minded smile.

She and Mr. Oakley certainly didn't look old enough to have an aging daughter. If only Charles could see Miss Oakley for himself. Was her father unaware that he was hiding her from Charles's view? Or was that his intention—putting off Charles's inevitable disappointment at the discovery of Miss Oakley's age and appearance?

"Come," Mother said, urging Charles farther into the room, "you remember Mr. and Mrs. Oakley, do you not?"

"Of course. Lovely to see you both again."

Mr. Oakley held no hint of a smile on his features. "And you, Mr. Shepherd."

Charles had met Mr. and Mrs. Oakley at Westburn last year after returning home for a few days. He had liked the couple well enough. Mrs. Oakley still had that unchanged distant look about her, but Mr. Oakley had appeared much less...examining.

Miss Oakley had been in Bath with her aunt at the time, and Charles had missed his opportunity to have met her—a disappointment only due to not overcoming this issue months earlier.

Thirteen minutes left.

"Thank you for agreeing to this," Mr. Oakley continued. "We are indebted to you."

Indebted? For Charles meeting his daughter? Was Mr. Oakley as desperate as Mother to see their children married?

His stomach tightened. Mother had to have told them of Charles's aversion to arranged marriages. If she hadn't, this was not going to end well for any of them.

"It is my pleasure to come here," Charles responded, as politeness dictated. He held his hands behind his back, clenching his fingers together to avoid fidgeting.

Mr. Oakley scrutinized him again.

"Son..." Mother paused with an anxious glance at Charles, "this is Miss Marie Oakley."

Finally, the Oakleys shifted to the side like a curtain being drawn, and Miss Oakley was revealed.

Well, she certainly wasn't fifty.

With her hair in an elegant chignon, dark curls gracing smooth, pale skin, and red, curved lips, Miss Oakley had to be one of the most bewitching women Charles had ever seen. She watched him with eyes as dark as the night's sky and a subtle smile that somehow caused her lips to appear even fuller than before.

"Mr. Shepherd," she greeted with a smooth tone, "how lovely to finally make your acquaintance."

Charles had to take a moment to recover. She could not be beyond much of his own age, and—as far as first impressions went—she appeared perfectly and refreshingly normal, holding herself with regality, though her eyes retained a kindness to them that was undeniable.

For once, Mother had not exaggerated.

He cleared his throat, shifting his feet. "Pleasure to meet *you*, Miss Oakley."

He'd been about to say more, something about how their parents were determined to bring the two of them together, or perhaps how pleased he was to see she was not an aged spinster or feral squirrel.

But when Miss Oakley scrutinized him as her father had, eying him up and down, Charles's words dried up. Had he passed muster? Unfortunately, her expression remained impassive.

Perhaps he'd extend the quarter of an hour. Spending a few minutes more with a woman who appeared as lovely as the portraits in the Royal Academy of Arts was hardly a chore. At least this way, he'd be able to satisfy his curiosity—and vanity—to see if he was a disappointment or a pleasant surprise to her.

Another moment passed by in silence before he realized all eyes were on him. Expectant eyes. Watchful eyes.

Right, he was supposed to be the gentleman here.

He settled his desire to pace across the room—an urging he had to quiet often in social settings, for the mark of a gentleman was stillness. "It is strange, is it not, Miss Oakley, that we have not met before, essentially living next door to one another? Although, I suppose it is to be expected, what with how often I am away."

"Indeed. Time and circumstances have certainly not been on our side."

She said nothing more, taking up her staring again as they all remained stiffly standing about the room. She didn't appear absent-minded like her mother, nor judgmental like her father, but Charles could see how deeply her thoughts ran, and he shifted beneath her gaze.

He didn't like how anxious she made him feel. He wanted a woman who made him feel loved, even admired. Not...intimidated.

Mother would tell him to give her a chance. But was that not what Charles had already done? Miss Oakley was beautiful. But already, he could see she was too withdrawn. Too quiet. Too... calculating. He preferred living life to its fullest, and clearly, Miss Oakley was not of the same breed.

And first impressions were always worth listening to.

"Unfortunately," he continued, "I fear our meetings will continue to be few and far between, as I do live a rather vagabond life. And that life, I have no intention of leaving behind quite yet."

It was as if Charles had called the woman a potato.

All eyes fell on him with varying degrees of frowns. Mother pulled back with a subtle but fierce shake of her head, Mr. Oakley's lowered brow nearly hid half his eyes, and even Mrs. Oakley's airy appearance shifted to slight confusion.

Could they truly be so astonished that he and Miss Oakley had not matched the way they had all hoped?

Miss Oakley was the only one who remained mostly unchanged, her eyes only slightly narrowing.

That put paid to it. He could never be with a woman who did not emote. Such a dull life, he could not stomach.

He fought the desire to pull out his pocket watch. Once again, a quarter of an hour seemed far too long. He might last another five minutes, but even that was pressing his patience, especially when no one else was speaking. What was the matter with everyone?

Father met his gaze, then subtly motioned toward the Oakleys once more. Apparently, Charles was the only one allowed to speak in this circumstance. Stupendous.

"So," he said, trying again, "lovely weather we are having."

Thunder rumbled outside.

No one made a response.

"Do you enjoy walks in the sunshine, Miss Oakley?" Heaven help her to know he was not requesting they do so together.

"I suppose."

He fought the urge to frown. She supposed? Who didn't enjoy walking in the sunshine?

A woman who was not for him, that was who.

He gave his parents a look that very clearly stated, *I am finished. I have done my duty. It is now your turn.*

However, Mr. Oakley spoke instead. "I apologize for the delay. You must be wondering why we have not yet begun."

Charles looked between his parents and Miss Oakley, confusion parting his lips. Begun? Begun what?

"I have already shared this with your parents, Charles," Mr. Oakley said, "but Mr. Berryman extended the time this morning by a quarter of an hour. He ought to arrive any moment now."

Mr. Berryman? The vicar? Why on earth was the vicar invited to their simple introduction?

But as Charles glanced at each person about the room—noting their looks of expectation and recalling their strange behavior—ruminations began to stir within him before pieces fell into place, forming a very unsettling picture.

"Mother," he began, his polite smile vanishing.

But his words ended as boots thudded outside of the door and Mr. Berryman appeared, holding in his hands a large copy of the Book of Common Prayer.

There was only one reason a vicar needed such a book in such a place, and Charles and Miss Oakley were clearly the main parts in this equation.

Blast it all. Mother had tricked him again.

Chapter Three

M r. Berryman moved to the front of the room near the Oakleys, a rather harried expression across his features.

"I'm terribly sorry for the delay," he said. "Thank you for your patience."

His white hair—balding in the center and thick on the sides—stuck up at odd angles and was untidier than Charles could ever recall seeing.

Mr. Berryman greeted the Oakleys and Charles's parents—avoiding Charles's gaze altogether—as he stood before the fireplace with his back to the hearth. Then he faced the six of them with a calming breath. "Now. Shall we begin?"

"Yes," Mr. Oakley said decisively.

"I think that would be for the best," Mother agreed.

Charles looked between them in stunned silence, still refusing to believe what he thought was happening.

Then again, he'd thought this before with Mother. When he was a young boy, he'd been tricked into eating broccoli with the promise of growing a full foot overnight. He hadn't grown a hair.

And then there was the time he'd been home from Winchester for the summer holidays, and she'd promised to leave for a fortnight with Father to London. She'd returned early, and he had been thoroughly punished for bringing a group of friends to Grendale Manor to hold a house party—or rather, a drinking party.

Tristan had gotten off without a scathing retort, which was just as well. He never acted out like Charles did.

There were countless other instances where Mother said one thing and the truth revealed opposite—especially in regard to the women she found to be "perfect" for him.

"Miss Beaumont has a five-thousand-pound dowry."

Yes, but the woman was already engaged to another.

"Miss Fitzroy is to inherit her family's extensive property."

Yes, but said property was in the middle of wetlands and would be shared with the woman's six younger brothers.

"Miss Grant has such lovely red hair."

Yes, but the woman was stronger than Charles and could throw him over her shoulder if he attempted to tease her.

But...*this*. This was the worst trickery Mother had ever performed.

"Miss Marie Oakley, Mr. Charles Shepherd," Mr. Berryman said, interrupting Charles's slew of memories. "Please, step forward."

Miss Oakley did as she was told, facing Mr. Berryman, but when Charles did not, all eyes fell on him. Father tossed his head toward the vicar, Mother nodded encouragingly, but Charles remained rooted to his spot and finally found his voice.

"I do apologize," he said, "but what exactly is going on here?"

He didn't really need to ask. Obviously, his parents had taken leave of their senses—no, they'd gone utterly mad.

Mother and Father exchanged concerned glances, then Mother gave a tense, little laugh. "Oh, Charles. You are always such a tease. But, son"—she cleared her throat—"I do not know if this is an appropriate time."

He stared at her, his mouth agape.

Mother meant well. He knew she did. And how he loved her with her opinions and pushiness and emotions. But sometimes, her will was unfounded. She couldn't possibly think that feigning ignorance would convince him to give up his entire life and marry a stranger.

A gorgeous stranger, but a stranger, nonetheless.

He looked past the scowling eyes of Mr. Oakley to where Miss Oakley watched him once more. No change had come across her features other than the kindness in her eyes shifting ever so slightly to confusion.

"Forgive me, Miss Oakley, Mr. and Mrs. Oakley," Charles said, "but I fear my parents have led you astray."

"Charles," Father's voice boomed from the background, "your mother was right. You must cease your teasing now."

"I am not in jest, Father," Charles said through clenched teeth. Then he looked at Mother. "Did you truly believe a trick of this magnitude would work?"

"This is no trick, son," Mother said.

Charles waved a hand about the room. "Then what is all of this?"

"Why, your marriage," she responded, her voice low as if the others couldn't hear, "to Miss Oakley—just as you requested."

Charles's jaw weakened. "*I* requested? I have never once expressed any desire to have an arranged marriage with anyone—let alone Miss Oakley."

Gasps sounded around the room, Mother's loudest of all. Father scowled fiercely, Mrs. Oakley's smile faded, and Mr. Oakley's lips were stretched in a grim line. Miss Oakley finally revealed her own uncertainty, her smooth brow slightly puckered, and for a moment he knew a sense of compassion for the woman who had clearly been duped as much as he had.

The only one who did not appear surprised was Mr. Berryman. In fact, he looked as if he'd *expected* Charles's actions.

The vicar had been over the parish since Charles was a boy. Charles had tormented the man during his sermons, whispering to Tristan incessantly and tossing pebbles at the vicar as he pulled faces—all while Mother and Father weren't watching.

Charles had repented of his childish ways since. Well, not so much repented as replaced his habits for less annoying ones. But Mr. Berryman had never liked Charles. Due to the condemning eyes now on him, Charles didn't find it difficult to believe the vicar's opinion of him hadn't changed.

But Charles refused to feel a shred of guilt. His parents were to blame for all of this.

"I must apologize for the shock this must be causing," Charles said, then he faced Mother directly, "but how could you do this? Not only have you tricked me into coming here and encouraged me to believe that this would be a simple meeting, but you've also allowed the charade to carry on for the Oakleys, as well. One can only imagine the damage this will cause to all of us."

Her chin began to quiver, and Charles grimaced. Mother could cry at the drop of a hat—and often did so—but she needed to know her behavior was unacceptable.

And yet, when Father moved forward in clear defense of his wife, Charles knew his words had gone too far.

"What on earth is going on here?" Mr. Oakley chimed in. "We deserve an answer."

"We all do, Mr. Oakley," Father said. "I assure you, we will get to the bottom of this." He faced Charles. "For the last time, this was no trick. And how dare you stand there and cast such accusations toward your mother when you know full well the contents of your last letter."

Charles stared. His last letter had been filled with sardonic and fictitious agreements. There was no chance it could have been taken seriously.

But as he looked about the room, each pair of eyes confirmed his worst fears.

"You said you had changed your mind," Mother said, leaning forward with her eyebrows drawn high. Her tears had vanished, as had her quivering chin—as quick to disappear as it was to appear. "You told me to make all the arrangements. You even set this very date."

"This miscommunication is precisely why God condemns any sort of untruth, whether speaking with satire or otherwise," chimed Mr. Berryman.

Charles cast him a look of long-suffering, then faced Mother again. "Tell me you did not take my word as fact."

"I believe one look around the room will help you deduce just exactly what she thought," Father said dully. "What we *all* thought."

If anyone had ever questioned whom Charles had inherited his wit from, the truth was now obvious.

Mother pulled up her reticule, rummaged around the deep pocket, then pulled out a crumpled letter. "Here," she said, thrusting it toward Charles. "Read this and tell me you did not mean a single word of it."

"You have it with you?" he asked incredulously, accepting the letter.

"It made me so happy, that is all," she said, dabbing at fake tears. "I like to be reminded of it."

Charles clenched his teeth, then read over the whole of his words, most of which he'd forgotten.

Mother,

Very well, you've convinced me. Arrange the marriage. Set the date. Order the flowers. Send out the invitations. Read the banns. Purchase a ring for her, will you? I care very little about the details.

As for the marriage date, that must be perfect. How about the eleventh of March? A nice odd number. Should be lovely weather, too. The rain will help ring in my new life with Miss Oakley. I will be home for a few days, so that will be just enough time for me to become acquainted with my new wife.

Oh, heavens above. I haven't the time to obtain a license. Perhaps one of you could do that. The banns must be read as soon as possible. Better yet, we ought to look into obtaining a special license. This marriage will be special, so why do we not forgo a church ceremony and begin our life with a license using the same descriptor as my and Miss Oakley's future.

Perhaps Mr. Oakley will be able to manage that with his connections, seeing as how he is the grandson of an earl—as you have mentioned to me at least half a dozen times.

But one simple request: might I meet my future wife first?

Charles

Charles lowered the letter, then looked at Mother. "*This* was not obvious enough to be taken in jest?"

"You were so convincing," Mother said defensively. "And seemed so serious."

"When have I ever been serious in my life?"

"Calm down, son," Father said reprovingly. "I also read the letter and was convinced of your earnestness."

"As was I," Mr. Oakley stated.

"And I," Mrs. Oakley agreed.

"That's wonderful," Charles said with a shake of his head. "I'm relieved to hear my personal correspondence with my mother is being shared for all to partake."

"It *did* pertain to them, son," Mother said with a sigh, as if Charles was the one being unreasonable.

He looked at Miss Oakley, expecting her to be embarrassed. Humiliated, even. He knew *he* would be, if he were in her position—ready to sign his life away to a person, only to find out that person had to be tricked into agreeing to the marriage.

But to his surprise, she remained stoic, still, and watchful.

"Did *you* read the letter?" he asked.

"I did."

"And..."

"And, what?"

Heavens, she was the least forthcoming person he had ever spoken to. "And did you think I was serious?"

"I did not have any reason to believe otherwise."

He studied her, still unable to read her. Why did she appear so unruffled with this whole matter? Was she not embarrassed, surprised, or disappointed?

Or had she been forced into this arrangement as much as he had and was now relieved there might be a way out of it?

"There, you see, son?" Mother said. "Your letter was so very convincing. Furthermore, you did not respond in the contrary to any of my other letters I sent, apart from the very last one."

"What other letters? I received nothing after I sent this, apart from the one that set the date. The date"—he swiftly added before she could speak—"that I thought was for my *meeting* Miss Oakley, not marrying her."

"Heavens," Mother said, shaking her head. "I am certain I sent them."

"They're not hidden somewhere in that reticule of yours?" Charles asked.

She gave him a very unimpressed look, the same he'd received countless times as a boy when he spoke out of turn or tracked muddied footprints across her newly remodeled parlor carpet.

"No," she said. "I sent them directly to Leonard Stanton's house, I'm sure of it."

"Whose?" he asked, leaning forward with his ear toward her.

"Leonard Stanton."

He closed his eyes. "Mother, I was not staying with him at the time. I was staying with Rowan Ashworth in Penwick."

She blinked. "Oh."

"How did you manage to send so many letters to the correct

location when the most important ones went to another?" he asked.

She pressed her lips together with impatience. "Honestly, Charles. How am I to keep all of your and Tristan's friends straight? There are at least a dozen of them."

"There are seven of us. Two of whom you've birthed."

She waved a passive hand before her. "You cannot blame me for mixing them up every now and again." She lowered her voice. "Especially when you live as a vagabond." She straightened, then smiled reassuringly at the Oakleys. "At any rate, the letters *were* sent, that is what is most important."

She was mad. That was all there was to it. Honestly, he wouldn't put it past her to have sent the letters to the wrong place on purpose.

"What exactly did you write in these letters anyway?"

"Well, there were three, to be exact." She raised her fingers, counting them out. "In the first, I told you that the Oakleys"—she paused sending an affectionate smile at Miss Oakley—"had agreed to the marriage upon your acceptance."

"My *alleged* acceptance," he inserted.

"In the second," she continued, ignoring his words, "I informed you that Mr. Oakley had, indeed, managed to procure a special license. And in the third, I told you of our shared desire to maintain discretion. That no one should hear of the marriage until after it had been accomplished, and that the union should be discussed with those around us as a happy one."

Charles stared. "So your intention was to lie to everyone we know?"

"Not *lie*," Mother said with a quick settling smile in Mr. Berryman's direction. "Our intention was to keep you and Miss Oakley safe from gossip by ensuring everyone that yours was a marriage of joy. At any rate, we did not believe that would be a stretch, due to your good-natured response."

Charles walked about the room, pacing back and forth and

running his fingers through his hair. "Did you not question my supposed acceptance when I did not respond to the others?"

"You are not exactly prompt with your correspondence, son," Father piped in. "In truth, you very rarely respond at all."

Charles glanced at the others, heat rushing over his cheeks. Mr. Oakley hardly seemed impressed, Miss Oakley remained unchanged, and Mr. Berryman, once again, didn't look surprised.

Nothing like his parents airing out their grievances in front of all the world to see. It wasn't Charles's fault he couldn't keep up with all of Mother's letters. Especially when more than half of them begged to introduce women to him.

Little did he know his lack of correspondence would lead to his mother arranging a *marriage* for him.

He blew out a large puff of air. This was too much. It was all too much. He needed fresh air. Space to move. Somewhere without six sets of eyes on him.

"Charles," Mother said softly, seeming to sense his overwhelm, "all of this letter business hardly matters now."

"It most certainly does matter," he stated, refusing to be mollified. "For everyone who expects the marriage will now surely be disappointed."

The silence grew so thick, Charles couldn't move now if he tried.

"Disappointed," Mr. Oakley said. "You mean to say you have no intention of marrying my daughter?"

Charles straightened. "No, sir. I do not."

Mr. Oakley took an abrupt step forward, but Charles stood his ground. Before the man could move any closer, however, Miss Oakley's hand shot forward, staying her father's advancement.

"Father, a word?"

Chapter Four

With sure steps, Marie pulled her father to the far side of the room, acutely aware of Mr. Charles Shepherd doing the same with his own parents so there was no chance of overhearing either conversation.

Mother remained beside the vicar, standing in silence with an unbothered smile, just like always.

"The audacity of the man," Father grumbled as she faced him. "To imagine he believes he can simply escape this union by his own miscommunication. It is unthinkable."

Marie nodded, soothingly. "I know, Father. But we must maintain our dignity. His parents are our friends, first and foremost."

"Yes, but how can I remain calm after he insults you so?"

"I don't recall any insults."

"His mere rejection of you is the highest form."

"I am not so very injured by that."

And that was the truth. She was well aware of the look of approval in Mr. Charles Shepherd's eyes when he'd first noticed her. In truth, she had been pleasantly surprised by his features, as well.

She glanced beyond Father's shoulder now, stealing another

glimpse of the younger Mr. Shepherd. He was as tall as he'd appeared on the drive, with a thick, dark mane and a shadow of facial hair already appearing across his jawline. Wrinkles jutted out from his eyes, indicative of how often he must smile, but his lips held no sign of anything other than a frown as he spoke animatedly to his parents, their own hands raised in order to quiet his words.

Poor man. He had clearly received the shock of his life. That being said, how could Marie consider his actions a rejection when he'd never agreed to the marriage in the first place?

"Well," Father said gruffly, "whether you are offended or not, the man will be made to follow through with the arrangement."

Marie hesitated, her mouth hovering open, the words on the tip of her tongue.

Father stared hard. "Do not tell me you have a mind to reject this proposal now, too."

"No, Father. Of course not. However, surely you can see circumstances have changed. I agreed to the marriage when I was under the impression that he wished to marry me. Now that the truth has been revealed..."

She couldn't finish her statement. Father appeared ready to blast steam from his nose like a kettle.

When plans were made, and those plans did not come to fruition due to another's actions, Father could hardly stand it, whether it was dinner parties falling through or trips being cancelled.

"Being reliable is important," he always said. *"Being trustworthy is even more so."*

She reached forward, placing a soothing hand on his arm. "Father, you know I will follow through with this wedding."

Instantly, his breathing settled.

"I was only saying," she continued carefully, "that there might be other options for me now."

Father stared, clearly shocked at the way Marie was not reacting—offended or otherwise.

It wasn't that she wasn't feeling *anything*. She'd never felt so many emotions all at once. Humiliation, relief, confusion. They threatened to overwhelm her, but she did as she always did in situations that unearthed her ground—took a deep breath, imagined standing before a calm brook, and moved forward with confidence.

"I'm sorry, but there are no other options," Father pressed. "This is your one chance at having a future."

So she'd been told for months.

Marie had never wanted to marry a stranger. She'd hoped to be able to remain with her parents and have more of a chance at finding a spouse she actually loved. Her parents were well enough off to live comfortably the rest of their days. Surely they wouldn't mind providing for her.

Yet, Marie had no desire to become a burden on them. Indeed, that was why she'd agreed to the wedding. Well, that and because she believed Mr. Shepherd had wanted to marry *her*. After all, finding a man who wanted an arranged marriage—a man who was not in his late fifties, to be exact—was becoming more and more difficult.

But now that she knew Mr. Shepherd wished for nothing *less*, she wasn't entirely torn up about having to change her plans. She had no desire to marry a man who responded in such a satirical way to a matter as delicate and serious as an arranged marriage. She far preferred a husband who could be serious, relied upon, and courteous—all of which Mr. Charles Shepherd was not.

"We have discussed this in great length, Marie," Father said, bringing her back down to earth. "A union with the Shepherd family will be your best chance at having a happy future."

Marie glanced at the Shepherd family. She had grown to love Mr. and Mrs. Shepherd in the last year. They were exactly the sort of people she would wish to be connected to—kind, caring, comforting. She'd believed she would feel the same way about their son. After all, the apple couldn't fall too far from the tree.

Unfortunately, while it appeared that Charles's apple did fall nearby, it was now rotting slowly beneath the great shade of his parents' branches.

"I love Mr. and Mrs. Shepherd," she said softly, "as you well know. And a union with their son seemed a good idea. However, I do not wish to *force* a man to be yoked with me. Surely we can find someone else."

Slowly, Father shook his head. "My darling girl. How I love you and your optimism. But the world is a cruel place, and men cannot look past the years a woman has lived."

Marie knew that to her cost. "What if my dowry was a degree larger?"

"We tried that before. None of it works. And you know as well as I if this marriage does not go through, your reputation will be ruined, and any hope of another marriage will be utterly lost."

It was the nail in the coffin she'd been trying to remove with her bare hands. But she couldn't. He was right. Too many people already knew of the special license they'd obtained. Too many people were expecting to see Marie happily wedded to the eldest Shepherd twin. Should it not go through now, who knew what manner of salacious gossip would spread about her, thereby ending *any* chance of a happy future?

"What are we to do?" she asked, forcing an unchanged tone and expression, though the favorable future she'd pictured was quietly slipping from her fingertips. "Force him into agreeing?"

She grimaced. How awkward—how terrible—to begin a marriage with a man pressured into it. He was to blame for this whole debacle. Lack of stoicism would always get a man into trouble. But she felt for him all the same.

"We must appeal to his senses," Father said. "Allow him to see what this will do to your reputation should he refuse."

"And if he still refuses?"

He looked at the Shepherds with a grim expression. "I shall take other measures."

Marie cringed. Father and his dramatics. She had no doubt he'd duel with Mr. Charles Shepherd if he were allowed to do so.

She could only pray it wouldn't lead to that.

She followed Father back to the hearth, waiting there in silence and doing her best not to overhear the last of the Shepherds' conversation.

"You will be happy with her, son," Mrs. Shepherd said. "Trust us."

"Trust you?" her son spat out in a whisper. "How can I trust you after all of this?"

"Hush now," his father said, motioning to Marie.

All three straightened from their hunched together positions, then rejoined Marie, her family, and Mr. Berryman by the hearth.

The younger Mr. Shepherd appeared no less frazzled than before, still running his fingers through his hair.

"My daughter was right to pull me away," Father began first. "She has reminded me that we are all friends, and friends we shall remain."

Mr. and Mrs. Shepherd exchanged glances of relief and nods of affirmation before Father continued.

"So moving forward, I should like to speak calmly, rationally, and with respect, if you so agree, Mr. Shepherd?"

The younger Mr. Shepherd nodded in agreement.

Father pressed on. "Now, I'm certain your parents have already shared with you the serious matter of my beloved daughter's reputation should you not follow through with this marriage."

Charles gave a firm nod. "Yes, sir. I was informed that might occur. However, as I understand it, discretion was advised for all parties included, so no one will have heard of the marriage but us. As I'm certain we six can hold our tongues and...Mr. Berryman?"

A look passed between the vicar and the man that Marie couldn't begin to understand. "A man of God always keeps his word," Mr. Berryman said.

"Naturally," Mr. Shepherd mumbled. "As such, no damage to Miss Oakley's reputation will occur if only the seven of us are aware of a marriage even occurring."

"Ah, yes," the elder Mr. Shepherd said from the back. "There is one small problem with that."

Mr. Charles Shepherd frowned. "And what is that?"

"Well," Mrs. Shepherd began with a small, sheepish grin, "you see, I was so thrilled at the prospect of you marrying Marie that I may or may not have let the word slip to a few...dozen people."

Her son gaped. "Mother..."

"Can you blame me?" she asked with a shrug.

Marie hid her smile. Mrs. Shepherd was an utter delight.

Unfortunately, her son was not.

"I may have let word slip, as well," Mother admitted.

"And with obtaining a special license—as you requested," Father added, "many of our relatives already know, as well."

Marie wasn't surprised. She hadn't a problem with any of them spreading the word about the union. Until now.

"Does Tristan know?" Mr. Charles Shepherd asked next.

"No. It was easy enough to keep him in the dark, what with his constant presence in London," Mrs. Shepherd said.

"And we prefer to keep him in the dark, as well," his father said next. "Otherwise he may stay away from home for longer if he fears we attempt to marry him off, too."

Mrs. Shepherd hid her smile behind her fingers, though her son stared at her as if she'd lost her senses.

"So how many people *do* know?" he asked.

"Let us say this," Mrs. Shepherd said, "if you do not wed Miss Oakley, the entire town will know about it by morning."

"How?"

"Because you are supposed to attend a ball tonight to celebrate your union, and everyone expects to see you both there. *Happy.*"

"A ball?" Mr. Shepherd exclaimed.

"That was *also* in the letter," his mother said with an innocent smile.

"Is this ball the one you wrote to Tristan of a month ago?"

"Oh, no, that is another ball you must also attend—one *we* are hosting."

"Heavens above," Mr. Shepherd continued. "First a wedding, then another ball. What is next, a revelation that Miss Oakley is pregnant with my child?"

Gasps sounded about the room, horrified looks from the Shepherds and a deeply disapproving shake of his head by Mr. Berryman. Marie forced herself to remain unaffected, breathing deeply to dispel the blush threatening to creep across her cheeks.

There rotted the apple even more.

"Forgive me," he said, seemingly aware of crossing the line of propriety. "I am simply..." He rubbed the back of his neck, ending his words with a sigh before facing Marie directly. "Miss Oakley, as this concerns the two of us more than anyone, what say you on the matter?"

Marie remained silent, thinking through whatever weighted words she chose to deliver. In not marrying him, she would be resolving Mr. Shepherd's dilemma but causing grief for herself and for others. In marrying him, she would be solving Father's problem while causing grief to one obnoxious but otherwise guilt-less gentleman.

But she would not be put into the middle of all this.

"This decision lies with you, Mr. Shepherd. I have nothing more on the matter to say other than I agreed to this union beforehand and am a woman of my word."

She expected the gentleman to pace about the room again, but all he did was raise his chin. "I am a man of *my* word, but no word of mine was given."

"The letter to your mother would beg to differ," Mr. Berryman said pointedly.

"Thank you, Mr. Berryman," Mr. Charles Shepherd said stiffly. "Timely comment, as expected."

"Always happy to help."

Charles didn't look away from the vicar, his scowl increas-ing. Heavens above. What sort of man was this to create a silent battle of wills with a vicar? And more importantly, how on earth could Mr. and Mrs. Shepherd have ever thought Marie and their son could be happy together when he was so...childish?

She was but two years older than he was, and already, she felt as if she was looking at a young boy who was pouting at what plates of food were placed before him at the dinner table. She wasn't happy with this arrangement either, but he would not see her whining about it like a petulant child.

"So what is it to be?" Father asked, clearly finished with the affair. "Will you fulfill your duty—though unexpected—and marry my daughter, as per our agreement with your parents? Or will you subject her to a lifetime of grief and a destroyed reputation?"

A lifetime of grief? That was a bit melodramatic. She'd be quite happy spending the next few years attempting to find another husband. But Father was right. The chances that she would be able to find a spouse now would decrease even more if Mr. Shepherd left her, essentially, at the altar.

Mr. Shepherd didn't respond for a moment, a battle clearly raging within him. "Could we not postpone this a week or two? Allow me the opportunity to come around to the idea?"

"No," Father responded at once. "You are expected at the ball this evening."

He turned to his parents, his shoulders dipping slightly. "And I am to simply throw away all of my future plans from this day forward?"

"Not throw away," his mother said gently. "But adjust them, yes."

Mr. Shepherd took to pacing the room again. "What if I was already in love with another?"

"Are you?" Father asked gruffly.

"No. But I do have plans to attend a hunting trip with Tristan in a few days. What of that? And of my future plans to visit my friends? Am I to simply give up all of that? All of *them*?" He didn't pause long enough for anyone to answer. "Of course I am. Because that is to be expected."

No one responded. Only the fire crackled in the hearth. Slowly, Mr. Shepherd turned to face Father. He was eerily still—something Marie had not seen in him until that moment.

"Very well," he said. "As I have very little interest in taking part in the duel I have no doubt you would challenge me to should I attempt to leave..." He stole a quick glance at Marie. "And as I could not live with myself knowing I took any part of damaging a woman's reputation, I will marry your daughter."

Both mothers in the room exchanged hidden smiles. The elder Mr. Shepherd sighed with relief. Father merely gave a firm nod. No one looked at her to see how she felt, which could only be a good thing, for she wasn't exactly sure *how* to feel.

She was relieved, certainly, to not witness Father dueling their friends' son. She also knew some degree of calmness knowing she would not have to find a spouse in the coming years. And yet, realizing she was to be subjected to a life with this sort of man filled her with trepidation. The only comfort she allotted herself was the knowledge that, while he'd made his decision to keep himself alive, he'd also done so partially to help maintain her reputation. That had to be at least *partially* admired.

"And you will agree to the other arrangements, as well?" Father questioned.

"What, more than marrying her?" Mr. Shepherd asked incredulously.

"Yes," Father stated plainly.

"Very well. What arrangements?"

"That you will do everything in your power to convince others that this marriage was happily agreed upon, that you will go to the ball tonight and appear as joyous as any newly married couple, and that you will attend the bridal tour already arranged for you, beginning tomorrow."

Mr. Shepherd's mouth dropped open again, and he swiveled toward his parents with a look that said, *"There* was *more?"*

Mrs. Shepherd merely waved her hand in a flicking motion toward Father. "Go on, son. Go on."

He closed his eyes, then drew a calming breath. "Very well. I agree to the arrangements."

"All of them?" Father pressed.

"All of them."

Tangible relief sailed about the room, everyone clearly feeling the emotion aside from Marie, for suddenly, she was overcome with sudden, palpable, undeniable disappointment.

So, she'd be marrying Mr. Charles Shepherd after all.

Pity.

Chapter Five

Charles stood beside Miss Oakley, facing Mr. Berryman as the vicar read from the Book of Common Prayer with a languid voice.

"Dearly beloved, we are gathered here in the sight of God to join together this man and this woman in holy matrimony. Therefore, it is not to be taken in hand unadvisedly, lightly, or wantonly."

At this, Mr. Berryman's eyes settled directly on Charles. Charles stared right back at the vicar, daring him to voice just how deeply he disapproved of this marriage—and of Charles in general.

Instead, Mr. Berryman continued, even slower than before. "I require and charge you both that if either of you know any impediment why ye may not be lawfully joined together in matrimony, ye do now confess it."

Was having no love for one's betrothed not reason enough? Perhaps one's reputation was more important than Heaven's will.

After another condemning look at Charles, Mr. Berryman continued.

Charles did his best to listen. He had heard the words before at other weddings. There, they had been filled with promise, hope, and love. Now, they were filled with dread, emptiness, and a falsehood he could not bear.

"For be ye well assured, that so many as are coupled together otherwise than God's word doth allow, are not joined together by God, neither is their matrimony lawful."

Miss Oakley remained still and silent beside him, just as she'd done all morning—back when he'd thought a quarter-of-an-hour visit would finally placate his parents to allow him his own future.

Little did he know that fifteen minutes would lead to a lifetime of servitude. He should've known something like this would have occurred. He knew deep down this had all been a horrifying misunderstanding. But he couldn't help but entertain the thought that perhaps Mother had simply chosen ignorance on purpose.

"Charles Shepherd, wilt thou have this woman to thy wedded wife?" Mr. Berryman continued.

Charles was only vaguely aware the vicar still spoke, his thoughts remaining on the woman standing beside him.

Why *had* Miss Oakley agreed to the marriage? He'd been so overcome with shock and frustration he'd not considered this until now. Was she truly so overaged that no one wished to shackle themselves to her? Or was it due to her less-than-enthusiastic personality?

"Wilt thou love her, comfort her, honor and keep her in sickness and in health, and forsaking all others, keep only unto her, for so long as ye both shall live?"

Miss Oakley certainly hadn't chosen to be single—otherwise she would be choosing to *remain* single. Had something prevented her from marrying, then? Had she some dark secret hidden behind her beauty? Some personality trait no one could look beyond? What on earth had his parents fettered him to?

"Charles," whispered a voice from behind.

He glanced at his mother, then back at the vicar, who watched him with an unimpressed look.

"Still not listening?" Mr. Berryman whispered. "Shall I repeat myself?"

"There is no need," Charles responded.

He knew what had been said—and how he was expected to respond. And yet, his tongue was bound. This was it, his final chance to make a run for it. If he ever wished for his own happiness and his own future, he would have to flee now before he vowed otherwise.

But he already knew he *had* to make the vow. Whether this was all his parents' fault or his own, Charles would not ruin this woman, nor her reputation. For what sort of life would he lead knowing he'd destroyed another's?

Curse his parents for raising him to have a conscience.

"I will," he finally stated with a firm nod.

Mother breathed an audible sigh of relief behind him, but he ignored it. She should not be feeling such joy at this...this farce of a marriage.

You've made your decision, Charles. Stand by it.

And yet, he didn't really feel as if he was standing at all. He felt as if he'd taken to floating about the room and was now watching someone else exchange vows with Miss Oakley.

"I will," Miss Oakley responded.

Charles hadn't even heard Mr. Berryman address her.

"Who giveth this woman to be married to this man?" the vicar asked next.

Mr. Oakley stood forth, and Mr. Berryman motioned for Charles to take Miss Oakley by her right hand.

Charles did so, but he could not meet her gaze, staring instead at their hands. Both were gloved, a physical barrier between them, and even still, Miss Oakley's fingers barely rested on his.

"I, Charles," Mr. Berryman prompted.

"I, Charles."

"Take thee, Marie."

"Take thee, M—" Charles hesitated. His mind refused to

focus. He'd said Marie, had he not? But what sort of name was that? French? Miss Oakley wasn't French.

Her eyes seared into him, but Charles stayed focused on her fingers still hovering above his.

"*Ma-rie*," Mr. Berryman repeated, speaking the word in broken syllables, as if Charles was eighty-five years old and hard of hearing.

Charles cast him an annoyed glance. "Take thee, Marie."

The vicar continued, and Charles didn't hesitate this time, repeating each phrase until Miss Oakley did the same.

To no surprise of Charles, at the end of the ceremony, Mother produced a simple gold band for him to give to his new wife, and he placed it on her finger after she removed her gloves.

She didn't so much as thank him, which was just as well. It was Mother's doing, after all. All of it was.

After the ring, no kiss was exchanged, much to Charles's relief, and no further word was spoken between him and his bride as the vicar prayed over those gathered.

Charles's legs grew stiffer and stiffer as the prayer continued far longer than it needed to. Finally, Mr. Berryman finished, and just like that, Charles was married to a perfect stranger.

And, coincidentally, a hundred pounds richer. He wasn't the last of his friends to be married now, that was for certain.

Still, the knowledge was merely a dim light in a sea of darkness he'd just committed to.

What on earth had he just done?

───────

Marie accepted the congratulations from her parents and the Shepherds, though she didn't feel as if she deserved it. Was it anything to congratulate when two perfect strangers made vows under pressure from external forces?

Charles—as she supposed she ought to call him now—didn't say a word to anyone after he'd forgotten her name. She hadn't been surprised by his hesitation. She was fairly certain he had never listened to a vicar a day in his life.

She tried to read his expression after the ceremony ended, but he continuously averted his gaze with a rigid shift of his jaw. Was he intentionally behaving like an entitled child, speaking so harshly to his parents and selfishly thinking of only how *his* life and future had been affected? He deserved grace due to the shock he'd just received, but then, did she not deserve some in return?

The next few moments passed by swiftly as Father urged Marie to return with the Shepherds to Grendale.

"No use prolonging the inevitable," he whispered to her with an embrace. "I am so proud of the woman you have become."

Marie was grateful to have her father's approval. Now, at least, she would be out of his hair. After all, what father would want his almost-twenty-eight-year-old daughter in his house forever?

Doing as she was told, Marie followed the Shepherds to the carriage awaiting them on the drive of Westburn. The rain poured around them, so the families said their goodbyes in the shelter of the front awning.

No tears were shed between her and her parents, nor did she expect any. The Oakleys were not a family who showed tender emotions—leaving room for more comfortable feelings like frustration or anger.

After an embrace from Mother, Marie walked with the Shepherds out into the rain, a footman shielding her from the waterdrops as he walked alongside her with an open umbrella.

She had only made it two steps down from the front stairs when she noticed Charles heading for his horse that had been brought around the same time as the carriage.

Mrs. Shepherd must have noticed her son, as well, for she called out through the rain. "Charles? Charles!"

He hesitated, then turned around to face her. His top hat covered his head, and the collar of his great coat was propped high to prevent the rain from draining down his back. "Yes, Mother?"

He really was a fine-looking gentleman. Unassuming eyes,

straight nose, quite symmetrical features all the way around. What a shame they did not match who he was on the inside.

"Do you not think it wise to travel with your new bride?" Mrs. Shepherd said in a lighthearted tone, though her eyes spoke far more firmly.

Charles stared at his horse longingly before stalking toward the carriage instead. "A fine idea, Mother."

Marie tried to stop her thoughts from running rampant about the man's behavior, but honestly, he was so *juvenile*.

Mr. Shepherd helped his wife and Marie into the carriage first, then he whispered to Charles audibly.

"This will make it easier for all of us, son. Allow us an opportunity to get to know one another, you see."

Charles didn't respond, entering the carriage last and taking the empty spot next to Marie.

As the carriage left Westburn House and bumped and bounced from the gravel drive to the dirt roads of the countryside, an awkward silence echoed loudly until Mrs. Shepherd spoke with a warm smile.

"Well, now we are on our way, perhaps we may relax a bit," she said.

Marie smiled in return, grateful for the effort her new mother-in-law was putting forth. Charles remained silent. He stared harder out of the window, his leg bouncing up and down in a disquieting fashion.

Could the man never hold still?

"I do hope this lessens before the ball," Mrs. Shepherd attempted next, motioning to the window. Rain pelted the glass, sliding down and blurring any chance of seeing much beyond the streaks. "There is nothing quite so agitating as trying to arrive presentably at a social event when one is sodden."

Marie smiled. "Indeed."

She glanced at Charles, though again he made no response. She had hoped he would have opened up when they were away from Father, but her optimism swiftly faded.

"When we get to Grendale," Mrs. Shepherd continued, "you must make yourself at home, Marie. You have been there enough to know where most of the rooms are."

Marie nodded, though not before hearing a subtle sniff coming from Charles that sounded suspiciously like a scoff.

"Your possessions, of course, have already been brought over and set up in your room," Mrs. Shepherd said. "Oh, that reminds me. Charles?"

His jaw tightened. "Yes, Mother?"

His voice was deep and rumbling, though it held a distinctive smooth tone that Marie could almost feel reverberating in her chest.

"You will not know this, what with your being at Rowan's house last month."

"I was with Ambrose in February, Mother. Not Rowan."

She waved another hand, clearly revealing how much she did not care what name she'd used. "Yes, yes. At any rate, I wanted you to know that we have moved you to the room adjoining Marie's."

Marie stiffened. Adjoining rooms were perfectly normal for upper-class, married individuals, but the thought of a mere doorway between her and this man was unsettling. And she would not even *think* about tonight. If the man couldn't even look at her, how were they to...

Well, never mind that now. She would cross that ridiculous bridge when it came. *If* it came.

"You'll find the room much larger, Charles," his mother continued. "It will more than suffice for your needs."

"Wonderful," he responded.

Marie eyed him sidelong. From the moment she'd met him, nearly every word from his mouth had dripped with sarcasm. Did he *know* how to respond in earnest? If only she'd met him before agreeing to wed. She would have been able to recognize the irony written all over his letter, thereby avoiding this situation altogether.

"I knew you'd be happy with the change, son," Mrs. Shepherd said happily.

Charles's jaw twitched twice, and Marie found herself staring for a moment, hoping to see the muscles flex again.

He may behave like a child, but he was a man in every other sense of the word. His lean shoulders and legs took up more than half of their side of the carriage.

"Now, Marie," Mrs. Shepherd said, "while your items have been situated within your room, you'll find that much of it will remain packed away in one of your trunks to prepare for your departure tomorrow morning."

"Thank you, Mrs. Shepherd. That is very kind of you."

There. *That* was how one responded to another's kindness, with gratitude and grace. Surely Charles had been taught as much. Did that mean he was simply refusing to be polite?

Give him a chance, Marie.

She flicked aside her conscience, but it continued to resurface. Perhaps all Charles needed was a bit of effort on her part, to let him know she was not a threat to his happiness—to let him know that a marriage with her wouldn't be disagreeable at all. In fact, their relationship could be quite pleasant.

She knew the physical appearance of a wife lent to much happiness for one's husband. She wasn't hideous to look at, nor did she have bad breath, so he would be well enough off.

Furthermore, she could encourage him to go on this hunting trip of his while she remained alone on their bridal tour. It wasn't technically a true bridal tour. Instead of traveling around the country, stopping to visit friends and family, they would be remaining in a cottage by themselves for a fortnight.

With Charles gone, she might get a little lonely, but she wouldn't complain about being left to her own devices for the first time in her life. Indeed, she might get a taste for it and press him to visit his friends—who seemed to mean a great deal to him —as often as he wished. Being away from him often would certainly lead to a better life than being near him and having to feign joy being connected to an adult-sized child.

She was certain they could make this work.

"Mr. Shepherd?" she began.

The elder Mr. Shepherd looked toward her with a smile.

"My apologies, I meant your son," she clarified.

"Oh, call him Charles, dear," Mrs. Shepherd said, catching on at once.

Marie glanced at Charles. "Very well. Charles?"

She waited until he looked her way, but he only did so by staring at her gloved hands on her lap. "Yes?"

"*Marie*," Mrs. Shepherd urged under her breath.

"Yes, thank you, Mother. I'm aware of her name."

She raised her brows. "Just making sure. As was the vicar before," she muttered under her breath.

He scowled. "I knew her name then, too."

She batted her eyelashes at him with a sweet smile. "Then use it."

Marie watched in silence as the battle took place before her, intrigued as the son finally relented.

"Yes...Marie?" he said slowly.

As sardonic and stubborn as he was, at least he knew when to submit to his mother.

"I was merely going to ask if you enjoy balls as I know your parents do," Marie said.

He looked back out the window. "I am not particularly fond of them."

Mrs. Shepherd frowned at him, but he ignored her, and Marie pressed on. "Does this mean you do not enjoy dancing or balls in general?"

"I cannot say I enjoy either."

"That is not entirely true, son," Mrs. Shepherd said. "I always see you enjoying yourself while dancing."

The corner of his jaw twitched again, sharply outlined just above his tall collar. "That was many years ago, Mother. I'm afraid I've lost my enjoyment for them. I far prefer being out of doors."

He paused, then shifted toward her. This time, his eyes focused on his own hands that had finally stilled in his lap. "Do you enjoy being out of doors...Marie?" he added when his mother gave him another look.

Heavens. How was she to respond now that she knew how greatly he enjoyed the outdoors? She shouldn't lie, but she had to find *something* in common with him to convince him his life was not over. Thus far, they only knew how they opposed one another.

Enjoying balls versus the outdoors.

Acting dutifully versus acting out of fear.

Expressing humility versus boasting pridefully.

Surely there was something they shared.

"I...*can* enjoy being out of doors."

"And what exactly do you enjoy?"

"As I said, I do not mind walking when the weather permits." That was true. When the temperature was perfect and the sun was neither overbearing nor absentee. "And I love picking berries." But that was because she enjoyed *eating* berries.

In truth, she was a woman born to be indoors. Away from stinging bees, sweltering heat, and soaking rain. Not to mention how miserable her parents made her when they did venture outside, always complaining incessantly about everything remotely wild until they were tucked away in the safety of Westburn's predictability. It had always been much easier to enjoy the outdoors through a window.

"Both very fine activities," Charles mused, then he returned his attention to the window.

"What do you enjoy doing out of doors?" she asked. "I have heard that you are a fine rider."

"I am," he stated. "But I enjoy all sorts of activities. Riding, hunting, fishing, sleeping, walking, breathing. If it is out of doors, you will most certainly find me there enjoying it."

Marie stared. What had her parents and the Shepherds been thinking? She and this man had *nothing* in common. The only positive note she could think of in all of this was that if he enjoyed being out of doors so often, they would be near each other far less.

Once again, the idea sounded nice in theory, but that had never been what she'd wanted in a marriage. Is that what he wanted?

Without responding, Marie turned to stare out of her own window, watching the water droplets race down the glass before catching Mrs. Shepherd's movements from the corner of her eye. The woman nudged her son with her foot, then tossed a head in Marie's direction.

Charles blew out a heavy sigh. "What do you enjoy doing indoors, then, Marie?" he asked with a pointed look at his mother.

What could she say that might excite him the most? She was frightfully accomplished—as was ensured by Mother and Father. They'd spent years pushing her to hone every talent she could, hoping it would lead to matrimony.

As if any of it had done her any good.

"I enjoy playing the pianoforte," she began, "and I have a particular fondness for singing, though I am not terribly talented at it."

"Oh, do not be so modest," Mrs. Shepherd cooed. "She is marvelous at both, son."

"Lovely," Charles muttered.

Could he not put forth the smallest amount of effort? *She* was doing so for both their parents' sake. If she were alone with Charles, of course, her patience would have worn out by now, but she had a reputation to uphold.

"I also enjoy reading," she tried again. "And stitching is a lovely way to pass the time. Parlor games are also riveting."

While Mr. and Mrs. Shepherd listened on with encouraging smiles, Charles merely nodded in silence. What the devil would it take to impress the man?

"What say you to adventuring, Marie?"

"Adventuring? As in…"

"As in partaking in adventures. The unexpected. Anything out of the ordinary."

She wrinkled her nose in disgust, then thought better of it. "Oh, yes. Taking part in adventures can be…riveting."

If one thought being away from the comfort of one's own home was riveting—which she did not.

He eyed her more intently. "Have you ever attempted archery?"

"Archery?"

"Yes. Archery. You know, with the bow and the arrow and the hitting of the target?"

She wanted to respond with some quip like, *"Why do you not stand in front of a target yourself, and we'll see how fine I am at the sport, husband."*

But Mr. and Mrs. Shepherd were watching, and she would not injure them with her words any more than their son already was.

"I have attempted archery, yes," she said.

"And do you enjoy it?"

"Enough."

"What about riding?"

"When the weather permits," she lied again.

Horses were fine animals, but Mother always protested about their height and smell, so her experiences with the creatures had never been particularly pleasant.

"Fishing?" Charles asked abruptly.

"I have never attempted fishing. It is more of a gentlemanly pursuit, is it not?"

He turned to face her more directly, his eyes on her hands once again. "Shuttlecock?"

Had he no response to anything else she'd said? "When one has the right partners, perhaps." She'd rather die than play on her parents' team. Father was far too competitive.

She swallowed to wet her throat, though she did nothing else

47

to reveal how unsettled she was by his constant spew of questions. This was an interrogation, one she could not win no matter how she tried.

How she wished to set forth an interrogation of her own.

"Do you know what it means to be a gentleman?"

"Do you realize you have the conversational skills of an ape?"

"Are you aware of just how deeply I despise you right now?"

"What of ice skating in the winter?" he continued.

"I suppose."

"Croquet in the spring?"

"I could be persuaded."

"Taking a rowboat onto a lake?"

"I have never done so before."

"Heavens, Charles," Mr. Shepherd interjected, both he and his wife watching the exchange with rapid eyes. "What are you trying to accomplish with all these questions?"

"I was simply attempting to get to know my wife."

"Well, get to know her in a more polite manner," Mrs. Shepherd advised.

"Of course, Mother."

He fell silent with a mirthless smile, then abruptly turned to look at Marie. His dark eyes delved into hers for the first time since before they'd married. "Thank you for answering my questions, Marie. It was most enlightening."

So, he'd been judging her, had he? Testing to see if they would make a match? By the uninspired look in his eyes, she was certain she'd failed. She was highly accomplished and willing to try most activities, but clearly, that was not enough for him. What more did he want? A woman who lied about her desire to be out of doors or a woman who touted her own accomplishments?

Whatever it was, she was certain he didn't want the *real* Marie. No man did—as was evident by her single status. No gentleman wished for a woman to admit that eating was one of her greatest joys. That singing in the comfort of her home was far preferable to adventuring out of doors. That her greatest desire was to be seen as who she was, rather than for her accomplishments.

She didn't know Charles very well, but she knew that any man who began a marriage by assailing his wife with a barrage of interrogative questions was not a man who would encourage her to be herself.

She tore her gaze away from him first, no longer allowing him insight into her soul.

He spoke again, remaining oddly still. "I don't think I'll attend the ball tonight."

All eyes turned to him in stunned silence.

Chapter Six

"Charles," Mr. Shepherd began, "you promised you would attend."

"I know," Charles said. "But a ball sounds rather dreary right now. And I'm exhausted from my travels. Perhaps I will simply take refuge in my bedchamber this evening and retire early."

The Shepherds exchanged concerned glances. Marie caught his gaze, his eyes holding a challenge she couldn't begin to understand. Was this his way of saying he wished to retire with her or without her?

She hoped it was the latter, for at this rate, there was nothing on this earth that would prompt her to keep her side of their bedchamber unlocked.

But not attending the ball that evening? She could certainly support that idea. She hadn't wanted to go anyway. Lying to all in attendance about her supposed love for her new husband was becoming more and more unappealing by every turn of the carriage's wheels.

Still, she would never hear the end of it if she didn't make an appearance that evening. Father would be furious, and Mother and the Shepherds, disappointed.

"You must go, Charles," Mrs. Shepherd said with a smile,

clearly attempting a more cheerful approach than before. "This will be your first appearance as man and wife, a celebration."

"That is just the thing, Mother. I do not feel as if there is much to celebrate."

Marie's tolerance of his childishness vanished. Of all the despicable ways to behave. The man was a complete reprobate.

"Charles, where are your manners?" Mother asked, shame in her tone.

"You are required to go, son," Mr. Shepherd said next. "You gave your word."

Charles moved his attention out the window, his jaw working ever harder. "Very well. If I must, I must. I will go to the ball, be on my best behavior, *and* ensure everyone believes our marriage to be one of love." He glanced at Marie. "However difficult that may be."

"I'm certain you'll find the strength you need to carry on, son," his father said threateningly.

Charles didn't respond. Marie pretended not to notice Mrs. Shepherd's apologetic smile in her direction. She was finished conversing. She was finished trying to get to know Charles and pretending to be happy with this arrangement.

All the Shepherds had said for months was how happy Marie would be with Charles, how much they had in common, and how wonderfully he would treat her.

Thus far, not a single one of their promises had been true. All Marie could think of was how terribly she'd been duped. And all for what? For their parents to get what they wished.

This marriage was not what she wanted. Not anymore.

Charles remained in the drawing room for a half hour after the carriage had arrived at Grendale, waiting for Mother and Father to join him for their customary cups of tea his parents always took after journeys.

They were showing Marie her new living quarters—and taking their sweet time doing so. Charles supposed he could have joined them. After all, his bedchamber would be new to him, too. But if he had to spend another moment with that conniving, sneaking, lying Marie Oakley *Shepherd*, he was going to truly unbridle his tongue.

He paced the room back and forth, his boots thumping between the wooden flooring and the red rug in the center of the space. He'd always felt quite comfortable in this room, its golden walls, white hearth, and red chairs warm and inviting. But now, all he could think of was how this space was to be shared from this day forward with his wife, whom he could barely tolerate.

He fisted his hands, attempting to dispel any pent-up frustration as he rehearsed the words he'd say, all about how he'd been tricked into this marriage, how he and Marie had nothing in common, and—worse than anything—how she'd lied in the carriage.

"Charles?" Father said as he and Mother, sure enough, entered the room a moment later. "What are you doing here?"

"We thought you'd wished to rest," Mother said.

"I do. But I must speak with you both first."

His parents exchanged looks, as if to give one another strength.

"Very well," Father said. "Sit with us, please."

"I am happy to stand, thank you."

Neither of them responded. Both were used to Charles's desire to always be moving in some form or another.

His parents sat down, sighing deeply before facing him with weary looks and motioning for him to begin.

So Charles did. As soon as the tea had been delivered and the servants had departed, Charles released everything as calmly as he could—how injured he had been, how unfair the situation was, and how frustrated he was with the entire affair. He expressed how they must not know him at all, for they never otherwise would have assumed his letter was in earnest—nor matched him to a female so unlike himself.

Throughout it all, his parents remained silent, which he was grateful for, as any defense on their part would have been rendered moot. This was, after all, entirely their doing.

"And then," he continued, "to discover the woman is a liar? I cannot bear it."

"Liar?" Mother interjected, speaking for the first time since he'd begun. "Marie is as honorable a woman as I have ever known."

Charles scoffed. "Then what do you have to say about her words in the carriage? She obviously despises anything to do with adventures and being out of doors."

"That is not what I heard," Father said.

"Nor I," Mother agreed.

"Then the two of you have been deceived," Charles continued. "How often have you told me we are alike? And in what way *are* we alike?"

"She *does* enjoy being out of doors," Mother insisted.

"And you both are trustworthy and honorable," Father said.

Charles shook his head. His parents had obviously been charmed by the woman's accomplishments so much that they could not see reality.

Marie had been lying clear as day about her love of the outdoors and adventuring—and the activities he'd mentioned. She had no desire other than to play her pianoforte and stitch indoors for the rest of her days, he was sure of it.

So how had she managed to lie her way into the hearts of his parents? Had she orchestrated this whole affair to trap Charles into marrying her since she couldn't get married on her own?

"There is more to life than your adventures, son," Mother said, setting her cup of tea down.

"I am well aware," he stated. "Like family and friends—like Tristan, whom I shall now have to disappoint by canceling my hunting party with him."

"Perhaps you could simply postpone it," Mother suggested. "Spend two weeks with Marie on your bridal tour, then take her with you on your little trip."

Charles ran his fingers through his hair. "She would be miserable, and would therefore make me miserable."

"Perhaps she could learn to love the outdoors as greatly as you do," Mother said.

"Stranger things have been known to happen," Father agreed.

Charles huffed, frustration overcoming him again. "You are both missing the point. Did you not hear the fact that she was lying to me? Does this behavior not cause you alarm?"

"She did not lie," Mother said, matching his exasperation. "She was merely stretching the truth so you might not be disappointed in her answers."

"Stretching the truth is as good as lying," Charles said. "Or must we ask Mr. Berryman his opinion on the matter?"

"You think he'd take *your* side in this?" Father said with a laugh, and Mother joined in.

Charles turned away, frowning. Father was right. The vicar had had it out for him from the start. No doubt he'd helped Marie with this entire affair, too.

"What am I to tell Tristan?" he asked pointedly.

"That you are married," Mother said. "Otherwise *you* would be stretching the truth."

Father hid his smile by taking a sip of his tea.

Charles shook his head, moving a few steps away and pacing the room once more. "Am I the only one with any sense around here? How am I to be married to a woman who isn't truthful?"

"Oh, and you are so very truthful all the time?" Mother asked.

"I am, yes."

"Really?" she pressed.

"Yes."

She dropped her chin. "What about the letter you sent to me, confirming your desire to wed?"

Charles stared. "That-that was entirely different. Satirical."

"Satire, truth-stretching," Father began, "it is all one in the same."

That settled it. Charles really was the only sane one left in this world. Did they not think he deserved an apology? Simple understanding? Compassion, even? Obviously, they did not. Obviously, they took Marie's side in all of this.

Heavens above. Was he *jealous* of the woman now?

He held his hands on his head, as if to keep his thoughts from bursting out around him.

"I cannot imagine how you even came to choose her for me," he said. "Yes, she is gorgeous. As perfect as a portrait. I'll credit you for that. But I care not for that or for her *many* accomplishments as much as I care about how I am now shackled for the rest of my life with the last woman I ever would have chosen to marry."

Marie had thought what she'd needed was to be alone, to rest. But being within the confines of her new bedchamber with only her thoughts for companions—with Charles no doubt resting peacefully a mere door-width's away—she could not find respite.

Instead of attempting to force herself to sleep, Marie left her chamber behind and went in search of Mr. and Mrs. Shepherd, as she always enjoyed their company.

She wandered down the corridor, reaching the bottom step of the grand staircase. Grendale Manor was much larger than Westburn House and her family home in Somerset—the home they left in order to travel across England in an attempt to find Marie a husband. How strange it was to imagine that one day, she would be mistress *here*.

Mistress with Charles as the master.

Childish Charlie.

She smiled to herself, heading toward the drawing room.

She'd concocted the little name for him after reaching her bedchamber. It suited him rather well.

Her footsteps were soft as she reached the carpeted corridor leading toward the drawing room, and her ears perked as she heard voices coming from within.

Blast. Charles was not asleep in his bedchamber after all. He was arguing with his parents, by the sound of it.

Marie turned directly around, not wishing to intrude. But more than that, she knew listening to Charles's grumbling would certainly not deliver the rest she so desired.

"A relationship between me and *that* woman does not stand a chance."

Marie's footsteps froze. She slowly turned to face the closed doorway of the drawing room, the voices slipping out beneath the crack at the bottom.

"She has clearly chosen to begin our marriage with deception," Charles continued. "Lying to me about what she does and does not like, boasting about her accomplishments, refusing to reveal who she truly is. It would not surprise me if I soon learned that she is the one who has orchestrated this entire affair."

Marie frowned. Leave it to Childish Charlie to even concoct such a preposterous proposition. She would have told him earlier how desperately she had *not* wanted the marriage to occur, but she hadn't wished to offend him.

Obviously, he did not share the same concern.

"She did nothing of the sort, Charles," Mrs. Shepherd said, her voice sharper than Marie had ever heard. "This was my doing more than anyone's, and with your father's staunch approval, I moved forward. Marie did not express a single desire or inkling to marry you until *after* she read your letter."

Marie raised a triumphant chin. *What do you think about that, Childish Charlie?*

"That blasted letter," he growled. "Would that I had never written it. I should have known you'd take your imaginings and run wild with them. You've been badgering me for years to meet with her. Little did I know I'd have less in common with her than I do a debutante!"

"I don't know, son," his father piped in. "Debutantes can be quite demanding, too."

Marie pressed a hand against her lips before a laugh could slip out. Silence followed, and she could only imagine the scowl on Charles's features as his parents no doubt beamed with amusement.

"You will find what you have in common, Charles, in time," Mrs. Shepherd said. "It may take work, but—"

"I do not wish to work to find what I have in common with my wife." His voice lowered to the point where she could hear just a whisper of sorrow. "I wanted a marriage filled with love from the first day to the last."

Marie's heart twisted. The pain hidden beneath all of his sharp words was apparent. She had longed for the very same but had given up hope the moment she'd read Charles's letter. Her parents had encouraged her to pursue the marriage, but ultimately, it had been her choice.

But Charles had been given very little choice at all—destroy a woman's reputation or ruin his future. And he'd chosen her.

Humility softened her heart. He may be behaving like a child now, but he'd behaved as a man when it had counted most.

"You will find that love and that joy," Mrs. Shepherd said. "I am confident of that, son."

"You may be confident, but I am not. Of all the women in the world, you had to choose her—a woman who is as lifeless and dreary as her accomplishments. A woman with as much personality as a handkerchief."

The compassion she felt before slipped from her grasp. She felt more the fool now than ever, having lent sympathy to the man who turned around and slapped her in the face with it.

The Shepherds instantly protested his words, but Marie did not wait to hear them. Her feet were already propelling her back to her bedchamber.

She had a mind to march straight back to the drawing room, demand an apology from Charles, and prove that he was wrong about her. But she knew the pain she felt at his criticism would cause her to become a blubbering mess. Even if she was a Shepherd now, she still had Oakley blood running through her, which meant she would maintain her dignity by refusing to ever cry in front of that so-called gentleman.

Instead, she would return to her bedchamber, make ready for the ball, and prepare mentally so she was ready to put on the performance of a lifetime.

Not for others, but for Charles.

She'd tried to be demure and polite, and he'd been bored.

She'd tried to let him know of her amiability, and he'd rejected her.

She'd tried to get along with him, and he'd accused her of lying.

And now, he said she was lifeless?

Well, Childish Charlie Shepherd had better secure his feet far into his stirrups. For if he wished for a wife who wasn't lifeless and dreary, he was going to get one.

Chapter Seven

M arie stared at her reflection in the drawing room window that evening. With only the fire in the hearth and a few spare candles lit nearby, she couldn't see beyond much of her outline, but having already examined her features in her bedchamber's looking glass earlier, she'd been more than pleased with her lady's maid's efforts tonight.

Jane had outdone herself, which was exactly what Marie had requested. Her dark green gown accentuated her figure in all the right places, and her gold and emerald necklace and earrings highlighted the hollow of her throat and her dainty ears.

Her hair was a true masterpiece, as well, her black curls stacked high and glinting with her every movement. A golden-colored ribbon embroidered with shimmering beads had been weaved throughout her locks with delicate intricacy, and a light brushing of subtle pink had been added to her lips and cheekbones.

To any outsider, she appeared every inch the blushing, glowing bride. Which was perfect, really. It was just what she needed to give her enough confidence to complete her plan for that evening.

She turned away from the window and faced the doorway expectantly, standing in the empty room with a quiet regality.

She'd been rehearsing her behavior and actions for the last few hours now and was more than ready to face her husband.

Despicable man that he was.

A few short minutes later, Charles appeared on his own, nearly coming to a skidding halt in the doorway when he realized Marie was alone.

His eyes scanned the length of her, and pleasure pulled at her stomach at the clear approval in his expression. He remained silent, standing in the doorway.

"Is something the matter?" she asked.

He hesitated a moment longer, blinked, then shook his head in silence. Entering the room, he headed in the opposite direction of her and toward the hearth.

All the while, Marie maintained a steady gaze. Charles looked dashing tonight. Pomaded hair, high collar, breeches that accentuated his muscular legs, and a green waistcoat that matched her gown. Whether that was a coincidence or Mrs. Shepherd's doing, Marie couldn't be sure.

"You must be looking forward to this evening," he said after a moment, his back to her.

"I am. I find balls a perfect way to discover more about a person."

"One would imagine talking would suffice in that regard," he returned.

"Conversing is unreliable."

Her clipped words pulled his attention toward her. "How so?"

"Any person can speak whatever they wish, whether they mean it or not." Her eyes honed in. "Actions reveal far more."

"Cannot actions be feigned, as well?" he countered.

"Not for long. In the end, a person always reveals who he or she is on the inside by their actions."

Shadows danced across his rigid cheekbones as he studied her, and a fleeting thought occurred about how this was their first time alone together. She'd certainly pictured the moment differently.

"So how do you come to learn more about a person at a ball, then?" he asked, his expression revealing that he had no intention of believing her either way.

Clearly, he thought he was in control of the conversation.

Childish Charlie, indeed.

"Sooner or later," she replied, "as the night wears on and propriety and politeness wane, the drink becomes stronger and the tired eyes become weaker, a person reveals his true character. How he treats others during those late hours is very telling."

He tipped his head to the side, eyes narrowed. "And are you hoping to learn more tonight about me? Or for me to discover more about you?"

She gave an enigmatic smile. "I suppose we shall simply have to wait and see."

His confident stance wavered only slightly at her pointed gaze, giving her further courage.

"Either way, I can assure you, Charles, tonight at the ball, you will discover that you have not married a *lifeless* woman after all."

She let the words dangle heavily between them. A flicker of alarm within his dark eyes shone first, then it shifted to embarrassment before he looked abruptly away without a word.

Satisfaction filled every inch of her. He knew that she knew.

Not a moment later, Mr. and Mrs. Shepherd joined them in the drawing room, complimenting Marie's appearance.

"Is your wife not utterly stunning, Charles?" Mrs. Shepherd said.

He peered down at his pocket watch, then tucked it away. "We had better be off. We oughtn't be late."

"Now who is anxious to go to the ball?" Mr. Shepherd teased.

"He no doubt cannot wait to dance with his wife," Mrs. Shepherd said with a grin and a wink in Marie's direction.

"Not at all," Charles said gruffly. "I am simply ready to be done with this whole debacle. I do not relish the idea of lying tonight. Though, I suppose some of us do not have qualms over such deception."

He looked in Marie's direction, though he did not meet her eyes. He'd found his voice, then, had he? Well, Marie would make certain he'd lose it again before the night was over.

"It is enjoyable to playact at times," she said with an innocent smile. "If I do well tonight, I think I might attempt to join a pantomime in London next."

Mr. and Mrs. Shepherd laughed, but Charles left the room, his shoulders stiff and unmoving.

"He'll warm up eventually," Mrs. Shepherd reassured her with a whisper as they filed out of the drawing room.

Marie nodded, though she held her tongue. The Shepherds were either in denial or completely oblivious—if not a bit of both. After Charles's temper tantrum that afternoon, they had to be fully aware of his feelings about the marriage. But she wasn't going to be the one to crush their reality by telling them how much *she* despised *him* right back.

No, tonight, she would be the perfect daughter-in-law, the perfect wife, and the perfect example of being filled with so much life, she could not contain it.

And Childish Charlie was going to hate it.

Charles stood on the outskirts of the ballroom, attempting invisibility amidst the crowds. He'd done a fine job of it thus far, having only danced a handful of times and succeeding in remaining hidden for the rest.

Still, this whole affair was beginning to wear on him. How much longer was he expected to feign merriment?

For as long as your wife demands.

His eyes tracked her as she danced down the set with her happy, smiling partner. He could have described every gentleman she'd danced with tonight in the same regard, for they all appeared delighted to be dancing with Marie.

Of course, she hadn't had a single spare moment to dance with her own husband. Indeed, she had not even glanced in Charles's direction once.

Not that he was complaining. Or jealous. That would mean he wanted her attention on himself, which he didn't. Walking into the ballroom together, forcing a smile with her on his arm, had been dreadful. Anything further would push him over the edge.

He was simply filled with indignation that she could be so happy with every other gentleman *but* Charles, and frankly, he did not approve of her behavior.

Were they not supposed to be putting on the appearance of a happy marriage? He was attempting to fulfill his duty—why was she not hers? Especially when she'd bragged about it so fully before they married.

Bitterness swirled within him—a bitterness that could rival his friend Leonard's. Leonard was persistently annoyed with his lot in life. Charles had always thought it humorous, but now, on the other side of it, the feeling was unnerving.

That woman. He would never again receive a single moment of peace being married to her. He couldn't even speak with his parents without her meddling.

At the thought of her overhearing his words, his whole body ran hot. He'd tried to feel better by telling himself that it was her fault. She'd been prying in on a private conversation.

But no matter how he spun the matter, he was in the wrong. He never should have stated such cruel things about anyone—let alone a woman he'd vowed to honor only hours before.

His parents had given him a sound tongue lashing after his words, and he'd taken it in stride, for he deserved every scolding word from them and himself. He was thoroughly and rightfully ashamed.

And yet, did any husband deserve *this* treatment—being

forced to remain at a ball in the back corners of the room while his new wife enjoyed the company of every single gentleman in attendance, apart from the one she tricked into marrying?

Her rosy cheeks, bright eyes, and bouncing black curls spoke measures to how greatly she enjoyed the attention she was receiving. Her glee was apparent, as was each of her companion's when she laughed with them, took their arm, and devoted all of her focus on each gentleman in turn.

Charles's jaw tightened, and he forced his eyes away, only to have them return swiftly of their own accord, as if they could not help but dwell on her disloyalty.

She clapped in time with the music and the other dancers, then spun in a circle around her partner before facing the man with more delight than ever before. The gentleman she danced with was tall and fair with blue eyes that watched Marie as if she *wasn't* married.

Charles's blood boiled. She had to be doing this on purpose. She'd experienced his cruelty and was now exacting her revenge by proving him wrong.

And she *was* proving him wrong. He'd claimed she was lifeless, and now, she was the life of the party. He'd claimed her to have less personality than a handkerchief, and now, she exuded character as she laughed, made her partners grin, and engaged in focused conversation despite their dancing.

And yet, Charles concluded that he was right in at least one regard—Marie really was as deceptive as he'd claimed. What other explanation was there for her frequently changing personality? And what other reason could explain why she hadn't been married? Everyone seemed to love her, so what had led her and her parents to ultimately seek an arranged marriage?

Mother had said Marie had simply never found anyone to love. Or was the truth of the matter that she had never found anyone to love *her*?

With her erratic behavior, Charles was beginning to believe the latter.

"Taking a moment of respite?"

Charles nearly jumped at Mr. Oakley's voice, having no notion that he'd come to stand beside him.

"I do not blame you," Mr. Oakley said without awaiting Charles's response. "Anyone would need rest after the day you've had."

Charles held his tongue. Were they to feign friendship now? Was Charles supposed to simply ignore everything that had occurred between them? He already knew he could not —*would* not.

"I find I must do so during social matters, as well," Mr. Oakley continued. He nodded politely to another gentleman and lady as they walked. "It was good of you to come tonight. Despite the rigors of the day."

Charles clasped his hands behind him. He didn't *think* he was in danger of reaching out to throttle the man, but better to be safe than sorry.

"I did not have much of a choice, did I?" Charles murmured.

Mr. Oakley cast him a sidelong glance, then sighed. "I should like to have a pleasant relationship with my son-in-law after all of this, so I shall begin anew and apologize for how matters escalated this morning—and for how you came to discover the arrangement. It must have been quite the shock."

Understatement of the year. Even still, Charles was minded to accept the apology. He felt more understood by this man than his own parents at this rate.

Still, his heart refused to be softened. "Thank you, sir," he said stiffly.

"I hope you know," Mr. Oakley continued, "had my daughter's future not been at stake, I never would have pressed for the marriage to continue." He paused. "I do not relish the idea of my child being married to a gentleman who does not wish to be married to her."

They fell silent, watching the dancers as they neared the end of the song. Charles didn't watch the dancers—plural—as much as he watched *one* dancer.

Marie's very nature seemed so innocent, so sincere. She was magnetic. But he knew better, and he wouldn't be deceived.

"She is a beauty," Mr. Oakley said with a nod in Marie's direction.

Mr. Oakley would be disappointed if he thought Charles had been admiring her as much as Charles had been judging her.

"You must be wondering why she has remained unmarried."

Charles pressed his lips tighter together. "I admit, the thought has crossed my mind."

"As it would any man. While I have no direct answer for you, allow me to assure you that it was not due to any scandal. Her reputation is spotless—ask any individual here."

Charles didn't need to. He'd seen the approval already. He may not have known very many people there, but the Oakleys obviously did. Indeed, the entire room seemed to love the Oakley family as a whole. No wonder her father was adamant her reputation remain unscathed.

A draught of doubt tried to snuff out the flames of his pride, and he struggled to keep it lit. Had all of Society misjudged Marie...or had only Charles?

He brushed the thought aside. All these people loving the Oakleys still did not explain why Marie was single. *Had been* single.

"We allowed the years to pass us by," Mr. Oakley continued, as if reading Charles's thoughts. "She spent a great deal of time with us, accompanied us wherever we traveled, and we enjoyed every second of it. But before we knew it, she had moved beyond the age of eligibility. Soon enough, interest—not in her as a person, but in her as a *young* wife—severely dropped."

Charles could believe that. Men loved impressionable, moldable young women. But he was more inclined to support the explanation that Marie was simply unlikeable. That reason leant him far less empathy for her.

"She is highly accomplished," Mr. Oakley said. "And she will make you a very fine wife, I am certain of it. I only pray you will understand one day why this has all occurred. I'm sure you will...when you have children of your own."

Chapter Eight

The words remained around Charles, a dead weight amidst the jolly music and happy chatter of the ballroom. He had been about to extend a certain level of understanding toward the man—no one could fault a father for looking after his daughter.

But the realization that Charles was expected to have children with a perfect stranger rushed over him with the heat of a thousand candelabras. He couldn't even stomach the idea. Such a responsibility ought to be done between a loving husband and wife, not...whatever he and Marie were.

Mr. Oakley left his side soon after the music ended, advising Charles to dance with his new bride before the night wore out, but Charles ignored him. He lasted a full twelve seconds before his eyes wandered toward Marie across the room again.

She was speaking with her previous dance partner—and a new gentleman who no doubt would become her next. She looked between them, throwing back her head and laughing at something the taller gentleman said.

Charles couldn't hear her laughter, but he could certainly imagine it. Grating, probably. Aggravating, too.

She proceeded to lay a hand on each of the gentlemen's forearms as she no doubt returned a joke of her own, and Charles scowled. He may not be in love with her, but they owed each other more loyalty than that.

She certainly didn't seem to think so. Was *that* why she hadn't married—because she loved flirting too greatly to be fettered by a husband? She'd gallivanted for too long and was now no longer amiable.

Her eyes abruptly connected with his, as if she'd heard his critiques, and shock struck through his stomach. He pulled his gaze away, but it was too late. He'd been caught staring.

He slipped behind a group of gentlemen near the outskirts of the ballroom, but to his regret, Marie appeared at his side a moment later.

"There you are," she said, slightly breathless, no doubt exerted by the pleasure she was receiving, dancing with every gentleman in the room.

She glanced around him at the plant he'd covered half his body with and the wall he'd been leaning against, then eyed him with a funny look. "Have you been hiding here all night?"

"I was not *hiding.*"

"Then what exactly have you been doing? Holding up the wall? Watering the plants?"

Amusement glittered in her dark eyes. For someone who had seemed incapable of looking at him before, she now apparently would not drop her gaze for anything.

Still, he refused to allow her to be in control of the conversation. Not when she was the one embarrassing them both this evening.

"I was merely attempting to exude decorum. Perhaps then others might know one of us in this relationship possesses the ability to do so."

Instead of scowling at him like he'd hoped, Marie merely grinned and faced the room. "If you believe sulking in the back of a ballroom is more polite than dancing, you are not as gentlemanly as your mother believes."

Wasn't *that* the truth. Mother had made her feelings about

him clear during her scolding earlier today. Had Marie overheard that, as well?

Heat rushed to his face. Before he could deliver a retort, an elderly woman stopped before them with a smile on her wrinkled lips.

"Good evening, Miss Oakley." She paused. "Oh, I suppose I ought to say Mrs. Shepherd now."

Marie shared the woman's light chuckle. "Yes, indeed. That will take some getting used to, I daresay. Mrs. Lewis, have you met my husband, Mr. Charles Shepherd?"

They exchanged pleasantries, and Charles pulled a polite smile onto his lips. It felt forced, like it did not belong where he placed it.

"I was pleased to hear of your marriage," Mrs. Lewis continued. "But I was disappointed not to witness it myself."

"Oh, yes," Marie said, tilting her head to the side with sorrow in her eyes. "I am terribly sorry. We desired a quiet affair. My wonderful father obtained a special license for us, and it all happened rather swiftly."

"Hmm," Mrs. Lewis mused with a wistful smile. "The youthful do hate to wait for the banns to be read when young and in love."

"Indeed," Marie agreed.

Charles's stomach roiled. How she lied so easily. Granted, her words hadn't been exactly untrue. She and both sets of parents *had* desired a quiet affair, and Mr. Oakley *had* obtained a special license.

But still, he could not join in, remaining silent until Mrs. Lewis departed.

"You are terrible at this playacting," Marie murmured the moment they were alone. "Though, I admit, I am unsurprised."

"And you are excellent at it," he retorted. "And I admit I am also unsurprised."

She peered up at him, but he wouldn't meet her gaze.

"Do you have a partner for this next dance?" she asked.

"I do not."

"Would you like one?"

His stomach dipped. Was she asking him? Why did that prospect simultaneously thrill him and fill him with dread?

"You could always ask your wife to dance," she finished.

Images of her dancing that evening flashed through his mind. "Have you not a line of gentlemen already pleading for the opportunity?"

"I do," she said flippantly. "But I thought I'd give you a chance to compete with them."

That was precisely her problem. She was under the impression that he wished to compete for her attention. Little did she know he didn't even wish for her attention at all.

Still, he had a duty to perform. He'd managed to escape Mother and Father thus far, but he knew if the night ended without them seeing him dance with Marie, he would receive yet another scolding.

"I will dance with you, should you wish it," he said with a heavy sigh that he hoped revealed just exactly how much of a burden it would be to do so.

"How very generous. Just for that, I shall promise not to bore you to death with my lifelessness."

She was clearly attempting to cause his guilt to fire up once again, and blast it, if her words hadn't produced the desired effect.

Charles was not one to care much about anything—aside from his friends and their adventures. He used to care too much about everything, and his life had almost been destroyed by it. Since then, and rather unfortunately, he'd learned to cope by masking any guilt he felt due to his apparent apathy by simply leaning into retaliation instead of retreat.

"On second thought," he said, "I think I'll forgo the dance altogether and leave."

His threat was empty, just as it had been in the carriage earlier that morning.

Apparently, Marie knew it, as well. She smiled at him, knowingly. "I thought you might. Well, you have made your appearance, and while your attempt was embarrassingly lackluster, I cannot fault you for it. Enjoy your ride home in solitude. Oh, and do not wait up for me. I intend to enjoy myself to the fullest this evening. Goodnight, Mr. Shepherd."

She began to saunter away, but Charles forced himself to remain steady. "You have everything worked out for yourself, do you not?"

She paused, turning around to face him. Most of the crowd advanced toward the dance floor, music signaling the beginning of "A Trip to the Clouds."

A couple walked by, and Marie nodded in greeting with a kind smile before drawing a step closer to Charles. "What do you mean?" she asked, her voice low so other passersby might not hear them.

He followed suit. "Your life. You have somehow managed to sort all the issues out so you have every happiness. You have a husband when you had no hope of obtaining one and a future when you had no hope of securing one. You have two parents who supported your intentions from the start, and now two new parents who dote on you at every turn."

Her smile lessened as he continued, and his courage took heart.

"And, having obtained everything you wished, you are now allowed to enjoy an errant existence of flirting and freedom. You've somehow managed all of the security with none of the loyalty. I tip my hat to you, madam."

Her eyes were as hard and dark as coal. "I do wonder if your parents are aware of how senseless their son is."

"And I wonder if your parents are aware of how treacherous their daughter is."

"I did not trick you into this marriage," she spat out, her voice raising before she checked it. "And as much as you like to believe otherwise, I do not have *every happiness*." She gave him a look up and down. "Especially now."

Finally, Charles had coaxed the real Marie from her hiding place. That knowledge satisfied him so greatly, he couldn't help but provoke her further.

"How could you not be happy?" he retorted. "You are secured for life. You have a husband who was raised a gentleman, and as such, he will provide you with all of life's basic necessities. He will ensure you are well cared for and bring you to balls to stand by in silence as you flirt your way around Surrey."

He'd hoped she'd hang her head in shame, perhaps even boast a blush, but when a satisfied smile reached her lips, his confidence faltered.

"You were watching me, then?" she asked.

Blast. "It is difficult not to notice one's wife behaving like a spectacle."

"Oh, so I am a spectacle now? What a relief, as I thought I had less personality than—what was it again? Oh, that is right—a handkerchief."

He cringed. Hearing his own words out loud managed to unseat his stubborn pride for a moment, replacing it with an overwhelming sense of embarrassment and guilt. He'd been raised better than to even entertain such criticisms about a woman, let alone voice them. No matter what Marie had done, no one deserved such unkindness.

And yet, did he deserve the unkindness shown to him by his own parents?

He stamped the emotions down within him, unwilling to harbor the unwelcome, vulnerable feeling a moment longer.

"I'm sorry you overheard my words from earlier," he began, "but you should not have been listening to them to begin with."

"Is that your idea of an apology?"

"Forgive me. I cannot lie as well as you," he said.

No hint of a smile touched Marie's lips any longer. The next dance had already begun, the excited chatter drowned out by the countless feet tapping the dance steps against the floor.

Charles was only vaguely aware of the fact that he still

remained in the ballroom, consumed instead by Marie's calculating gaze.

"I might have believed you before," she said. "That you were incapable of lying. But this evening, just as I suspected, your true character has been revealed. You were merely performing before, just like the rest of us."

"Was I?"

"Yes. Not only have you deceived your parents into thinking you are a gentleman, but you have also convinced *yourself* that your charm and status are enough to make a woman happy in an unwanted arranged marriage—simply because it is a marriage with *you*. But let me assure you, Charles Shepherd. You are the last man I would have *ever* chosen for myself."

Her words cut past his pride, slicing through his insecurities and piercing the truth. She was right. About everything.

"I see past your performance," she continued, drawing a step closer to him, her voice dangerously low. "I see who you truly are —a spiteful scoundrel hidden behind fine clothing and polite words. You, Charles Shepherd, are nothing more than a child."

She spun around to leave, but that final word sealed up his wound, released Charles's pride from its maimed cage, and filled him with anger. He reached out, catching her wrist.

With a fierce scowl, she whirled around to face him. "Let me go."

"Or what?" he countered.

She glanced around them with a wary eye. "I shall tell my father. Or your mother."

"What can they do?" He pulled her toward him, and she stumbled forward a step. "You are legally mine now, remember?"

Disgust crossed her features. With a swift toss of her head, she motioned to his fingers around her wrist. "I belong to no one. And *you* swore to feign a happy marriage."

"Who is to say I am not holding you out of joy?"

"Your hardened gaze would suggest otherwise, sir. Let me go."

Charles fought with his conscience. He did not wish to harm

her—indeed, if she wrenched free, he would certainly release her
—but he was so furious, so livid, his fingers refused to lessen their
hold.

She was but two years his senior. How dare she call him a
child?

You have *behaved like a child today, Charles.*

That inner doubting voice slithered through his thoughts and
pressed him to maintain his hold of her.

"I will not let you go, Marie," he said. "For you have accused
me of being a child, and I am minded to prove you otherwise."

She scoffed. "How ever will you manage that?"

He forced his breathing to remain level. "By reminding you
that I am a true gentleman. And true gentlemen always keep their
word." He stared down at her. "As you said, I have promised to
maintain the appearance of a happy marriage, so I think I'll do
just that."

Uncertainty flickered in her expression. "How?"

He didn't answer. Instead, he shifted his hold of her wrist to
grasp her hand instead, then with abrupt movements, he
progressed through the ballroom, pulling her swiftly behind him.

"What are you doing?" she whispered, plastering a smile on
her lips as she nodded at the curious glances from the people they
walked by.

"I am doing what husbands do."

"And what is that?"

"Spending time alone with my wife."

Chapter Nine

M arie's heart was in her throat. They left the ballroom behind, heading in the direction of the doors open to the darkness outside.

She did not attempt to pull away from his touch, determined to maintain composure, though she was grateful to no longer force her smile as they left the ballroom behind.

"This is entirely inappropriate, Mr. Shepherd," she whispered through clenched teeth as they moved down the steps and farther into the gardens below.

"Not *entirely*," he returned. "At least not for married couples."

Giggles and gasps from nearby couples drifted toward her, but she could not see another soul. Could they see *her* being dragged by this man-child to who-knew-where?

"People will talk," she tried again.

"About how we are married? Is that not what you wished for?"

He continued blazing forward, their crunching footsteps on the gravel pathway punctuating the still, night air. Soon, the hedges he pulled her toward grew so tall, only the starry sky was visible above. Fortunately, the light of the moon lit just enough of their pathway forward.

Charles's broad shoulders shifted side to side as he pulled her deeper into the gardens until they reached a dark corner of the twisting shrubs.

There, Charles whirled around to face her, finally releasing his hold. The powdery scent of lilac on the breeze and the distant splashing of water marked the air, but Marie could not see anything beyond Charles's fierce glower peering closely down at her.

"Why have you brought me out here?" she demanded, refusing to be intimidated by his actions.

"Are you frightened?"

"Not in the slightest," she said. "I was merely wondering if I ought to prepare myself for you to make another scene like you did in the ballroom."

Honestly, there *had* been no scene. She knew her smile had been enough to convince any observer that all was well between the newlyweds. She'd just been wanting to deliver another swipe at Charles.

The music from the ballroom drifted on the breeze toward them, and she fought the urge to flee toward the joy she'd felt before. The knowledge that Charles had been watching her, becoming jealous at her attention toward other men, had nourished her starving pride.

But now, she feared she may have taken a bite too large. Charles's expression retained an unhinged look, the fury in his eyes visible in the light of the moon.

Marie truly wasn't frightened of him. Even when he'd held her wrist, his grasp had been soft enough to allow her to get away if she'd truly tried. She just hadn't wanted to make a scene. And, furthermore, were Charles *truly* a violent man, he certainly would not have hesitated to throttle her by now.

Even still, she *was* uneasy because she didn't know what to expect from him out here.

"I was not making a scene," he stated. "I was—am— attempting to adjust to the idea of what my future holds now and what my present is. The events of today have rocked my stability past the point of logic."

"Do you not think my own stability has been rocked?" she countered.

"You have had far longer than I to adjust to it."

"Yes, but I have had far shorter a time to adapt to my discovery of marrying a child who resorts to throwing a fit when he does not get his way."

"I am no child," he said, stating each word carefully.

That was the word she'd used before to push him over the edge. *Child.* Dare she continue? Goading was no way to treat one's husband.

"..as lifeless and dreary as her accomplishments...as much personality as a handkerchief."

Fire burst within her. That answered that, then.

"Are you *not* a child?" she challenged.

She was pushing him, and even though she knew she was being childish herself, there was a fire and a passion in their conversation she'd never experienced herself—nor had she ever witnessed in anyone. All of her frustrations were spilling forth upon him, kindling to his already raging fire, and with each new flame produced, she received a boost of satisfaction.

And blast it all, if she didn't wish to stroke her morbid curiosity further to see just what he might say next.

She drew a step closer to him, giving in to her human failings. "Then what would you call storming out of a ballroom simply because you did not like the words coming from my lips?"

His eyes centered on her mouth, his broad chest rising and falling with angry breaths. "I had to leave before a *true* scene would be made. Some would call that self-control and compassion."

"I would call it unable to be domesticated."

His nostrils flared, and he took an abrupt step toward her. She did not flinch, merely lifting her chin to meet his gaze and whatever further vitriol he would let loose.

But nothing more came.

Instead, he closed his eyes, a line forming in the middle of his brow as he created more distance between them.

"This was your plan all along, was it not?" he asked. "To trick my parents into thinking you are amiable and accomplished so they would arrange for you to marry me."

"Are you truly so prideful as to believe I wished to marry you so desperately?" she asked.

"No, of course not. Because any man would do for you, wouldn't he?" His eyes found hers again. "You cared not who you'd wed, so long as your future was secured. So long as you could dupe unsuspecting parents like my own."

Her heart twinged. She loved Mr. and Mrs. Shepherd—and that love had only grown in the last few months. Did Charles truly think her capable of taking advantage of their goodness?

"You do not know of what you speak," she said.

"Do I not?" He drew toward her again until she had to crane her neck to maintain eye contact. "Then am I wrong to assume that you've orchestrated everything because you knew you could not get married without my parents' approval, and you found my mother to be an easy target?" He took another step closer. "How dare you use her? Are you truly so selfish, so deluded that you thought you'd get away with—"

Marie snapped. Hurt and anger surged through her so swiftly, it took control of her limbs, bringing her hand up to strike the words straight from Charles's mouth.

Only he was too fast. He reached out with a firm grip around her wrist again, stopping her palm from contacting his cheek at the last moment.

He glowered down at her, his voice slower than before. "Is this how you wish our marriage to begin, madam?"

"Is this how *you* wish our marriage to begin?" she returned, motioning toward him with a shift of her chin.

They remained there for a moment, unmoving. A mere step separated them as his eyes delved into hers. Then his gaze dropped to her lips.

Marie's heart stuttered as his brow flinched, and his own lips parted.

Fear sprung within her at the mere thought of what might occur, so she hardened her soul and raised her chin ever higher.

"Release me," she whispered vehemently.

Charles hesitated, then did as he was told. Instantly, she backed away, holding her wrist to her chest and rubbing it as if he'd hurt her, though the burning sensation lingered due to his touch, rather than his grip.

He watched her actions for a moment, and she thought she saw a hint of regret in his eyes, but she didn't care. Not anymore.

"I will say this one final time, Charles, for your benefit alone. No trickery nor deception was had on my part in this entire affair. I am a victim like you—if not more so. I was not desperate to marry, but I *was* anxious to please both of our parents, for I have come to love your mother and father as if they were my own. You may believe what you wish, but I will not speak to this matter again."

He studied her. "How am I to know what to believe when you appear to change your personality every moment I see you?"

Marie squared her shoulders. "Why would I ever reveal to you who I truly am if you are simply to reject that version of me, too?"

His gaze dropped as he shifted his footing.

"I will return to the ball now," she said calmly. "For I believe these dances will be the last enjoyment I will experience for the foreseeable future. I shall tell your parents you will be leaving early. You may rest assured, I will behave myself. Excuse me."

She walked away, slightly on edge at the thought of him stopping her again, but he remained still. She moved beyond the lilac bushes, pretending to know her way around the hedges, though as the sound of the music from the ball grew softer, she hesitated.

Turning beyond another hedge, she came face-to-face with

the fountain, which was in the opposite direction of the house. Concern welled within her. She shouldn't have walked away alone —especially not in the darkness. She had no idea where she was going.

"I am staying."

Charles's words behind her caused her to jump, and she whirled around to face him.

"What do you mean by stalking up to me like that?" she said, raising a calming hand to her throat. "You scared me half to death."

"My apologies," he said. His tone was far less aggressive than before, but still not entirely sincere.

"Staying where?" she asked, referring to his words from before.

"At the ball."

"Why?"

"Because it is my duty."

She dropped her hand. "*Now* you're concerned about your duty?"

He delivered a frustrated sigh. "Why must you say things to aggravate me just as I've managed to calm down?"

"Why must it take you so long to calm down?" she returned.

He looked away. "It typically does not. But today has set my life into upheaval."

His tone fell, his demeanor shifting as he turned away from her and rubbed the back of his neck. "You made the wrong turn just there. Allow me to escort you safely back indoors."

His voice was soft, his shoulders slightly hunched forward, and Marie couldn't help but stare. She'd done it. Her words had finally broken through his tough exterior. She ought to celebrate, really. Smile haughtily as they returned to the ballroom and tout her winnings by dancing with every other handsome man in the room.

But instead, all she could think of was how much she

regretted stooping to this man's level by injuring him with her words—as he'd done with her.

Still, her pride smarted too deeply to apologize. "Why did you bring me out here?" she asked.

He continued rubbing the back of his neck, his fingers sliding behind his cravat as if he were attempting to loosen it. "Truthfully? I wished to shout at you without the chance of my mother overhearing."

Marie huffed out a scoff. "I should have expected that."

"Why?"

"Because you haven't exactly behaved honorably since our meeting, have you?"

"And you have?" he questioned.

"More so than you in the last twelve hours."

"And what exactly have I done that is so dishonorable?"

She held out her fingers, distinctly aware that their argument was gaining steam once again. "Let us count the ways. First, you wrote a letter to your dear mother using sarcasm"—she coughed out the word "lying" before continuing—"Second, you accused her and your father of trickery. Third, you accused *me* of trickery. Fourth, you claimed that your new bride was lifeless, dreary, and had less personality than a handkerchief. Fifth, you—"

"All right, all right," Charles interrupted with a wave of his hand. "This is entirely unnecessary."

"Yes, because you know I am right," she stated with a little wiggle of her head in victory.

He narrowed his eyes, shifting his body to face her more fully. Where they stood near the fountain, the hedges had parted way, allowing the moon's light to pour more brightly upon them.

"Shall we count how you have behaved dishonorably, then?" he asked.

"By all means. Enlighten me."

He took a step toward her. "First, you hid your true self from me before our marriage." He paused, coughing out the word, "lied," just as she had done, then took another step in her direction. "Second, you hid your true self from me in the carriage. Third, you eavesdropped on a private conversation between me and my parents. Fourth, you danced and flirted with every single gentleman in the room just for attention."

He paused, giving her a pointed look, as if waiting for her to deny her actions. But she was woman enough to stand her ground and *not* deny the truth when it was placed before her. Even if it made her sound like a wretch.

"Fifth," he continued, drawing ever closer, "you shouted at your husband in the middle of the ballroom—"

"You provoked me, and you know it," she cut in defensively. "And I did not shout."

"—and sixth..." He paused, staring down at her, a mere foot between them now. His eyes flicked the length of her features, and when he spoke again, his voice held a distinctive rugged tone that hadn't been there before. "You believed I would bring you out here to make good on my promise that everyone would know us to be husband and wife."

Marie froze. She could not deny the truth in his words. Her first thought had been that Charles was going to have his way with her. But how did that make *her* dishonorable and not *him*?

She was about to ask that very question, but as he dipped his chin to meet her gaze more fully, the air between them tangibly shifted. Where once, hostility filled the space, a sudden sparkling occurred, and her heart stamped against her chest.

"I doubt there will be a question in anyone's mind after you've dragged me out here, sir," she stated.

"Should we just be...certain?"

He wet his lower lip, and Marie reeled. How were they shouting moments before—so ferociously that she'd longed to strike him—and now, they were speaking of...this?

All confusion fled when she caught the look in his eye, the challenge within them, as if he were attempting to beat her in their repartee. Clearly, he intended to win this conversation, and he was going to stop at nothing to do so.

A fire sparked within her. She had never been a gracious loser.

He took another step closer, but her hand shot forth, planting between them with a halting movement. "That is close enough, sir."

"Or..." he prompted.

She took a subtle step back, but the heel of her slipper came in contact with the solid side of the fountain.

"Or I risk falling into the fountain and being soaked through for the rest of the ball."

He eyed her up and down, then raised a shoulder. "It could only be an improvement."

Marie knew he lied. She'd seen the look of approval in his eyes each time he stared at her—indeed, she'd seen it for the better part of the evening. But his very nerve at even stating such a thing needed to be checked.

He tried once more to draw closer, so she pressed her hand firmly against his waistcoat, intent on pushing him away to reveal just how much leeway she was going to allow him this evening.

However, with his firm footing and her severe underestimation of how solid his chest was, Marie ended up pushing herself back instead, and she lost balance. Her lower legs pressed up against the fountain wall and her hands spun out at the side of her like the wheels of a cart as she attempted to catch her balance.

She yelped, ready to plunge into the cold water behind her when Charles's arms wrapped around her and pulled her back to solid footing, slamming her body against his firm frame.

She breathed heavily, attempting to gain her bearings.

"You must be more careful," Charles growled.

She pulled back. He had some nerve to be upset with her for such an accident. "You are impossible, Charles."

"As are you, *Miss Oakley*."

"Are you so deluded that you've forgotten what has occurred this morning? I am no longer Miss Oakley."

He leaned down closer so they were face-to-face. "We'll see."

The threat in his eyes, the hidden meaning behind his words, confused her for one moment before riling up another wave of utter infuriation.

He dared threaten her? To what, get a divorce? An annulment? Whatever it was, indignation, annoyance, and anger fused within her. He expected her to buckle, to relent, to cave.

Well, Childish Charlie had met his match in Immovable Marie.

Her hands found the lapels of his jacket, and with swift movements, she pulled him toward her. Standing on the tips of her toes, she pressed her lips to his, and all of a sudden, she was kissing Charles Shepherd.

Her *impossible* husband.

Chapter Ten

C harles froze. What on earth was happening right now? Was this devil woman—this vexing, confusing, gorgeous wife of his truly kissing him?

Marie's lips pressed more firmly against his as if hearing his confusion, and her small fists clenched his lapels ever tighter as she tried to pull him closer.

He did not budge. In fact, his instinct was to immediately set her aside. He was not in the habit of kissing women he barely knew—especially women who threw themselves upon him. But when Tristan's voice echoed in his mind, he paused.

"You are being kissed by a beautiful woman—who instigated the affection, by the way—and you're not kissing her back? Are you stupid?"

Tristan—or Imagined Tristan—had a point. Charles had every right to kiss his wife back. And if Marie thought she'd get the better of this conversation by ending it with a kiss started by *her*, she was sorely mistaken.

"Are you going to kiss her back or not?"

Fine, Tristan. Fine.

It took but half a moment for Charles to respond. In one movement, he swooped his right arm around her, eliciting a gasp from her that broke their kiss for a moment. He pressed his hand to the small of her back, pulling her flat against his body. With his free hand, he slid his fingers just above the nape of her neck, guiding her lips back to his.

From that point forward commenced the strangest kiss Charles had ever experienced. Both he and Marie seemed to be taking part in a silent challenge of who would relent first—who would be the victor and who would be the failure.

Their lips moved together in a heated pitch, their breathing ragged and lips desperate to maintain contact. Marie's arms wrapped securely around his neck as her chest rose and fell heavily against his own.

Despite the strangeness of it all, it wasn't entirely unpleasant. Marie was so petite, fit so perfectly in his arms that he found himself pondering how greatly he would enjoy kissing her if they were *not* in a challenge—had they *not* been forced to marry one another.

He grew breathless with their feverish kisses, but something else contributed to it, an opening inside him, a swirling warmth in the center of his chest that could not be stamped out.

In truth, if he'd discovered Miss Marie Oakley at a ball that he'd attended of his own accord, he had no doubt in his mind he would have approached her without question, begged her for a dance, then spent the rest of the evening pining for another chance at being near to her. Then, if he had been truly mad, he would have pulled her out into that garden and held her just like this, only with *soft* kisses and caresses.

The idea of treasured affection between them lingered in his mind, and the change happened so gradually, Charles remained unaware of it at first. The frantic fervor between them lessened, the fever cooling into a subtle warmth that bloomed like a snowdrop within his heart.

Why had her kiss softened? Or had his thoughts caused his own lips to temper first? Either way, his breathing shallowed, and something shifted in their movements.

Instead of clinging to one another with desperate grappling, their grips softened, and their surroundings became more poignant and noticeable.

The water beside them gently rushed and gurgled, and crickets chirped their songs nearby. The cool spring air ruffled Marie's skirts against his legs and pulled one of her ringlets to tickle his cheek.

Marie's arms no longer held a vice grip around him, her fingers loose as they slid up the back of his neck. A small, pleasant shiver ran across his skin. Charles still held her firmly against him, his hands splayed out at the small of her back and between her shoulders, but in a coaxing manner, not controlling. When his fingers slowly shifted to rest at her waist, a soft sigh slipped from her lips.

Charles's heart hammered against his chest at the sound.

Were the two of them actually enjoying this kiss? There was no question they were. Their mouths moved slowly, working together instead of in opposition, as if they both knew that relenting just a degree would allow them both far more pleasure.

And, heavens, did it. His chest ached at the beating it took from his heart, and the desire he felt to deepen their kiss pooled deep in his belly.

Charles had never enjoyed a kiss as greatly as this—a fact he would be sure to never admit to anyone. *Especially* Marie.

She wouldn't admit to taking pleasure in it, either, though there was no denying the way she melted into him, as if her legs had given way and she expected him to support her, to hold her.

And he would. Just as he'd promised to do that morning as they'd exchanged vows.

Vows. Because they were married.

The realization of what he was doing struck him, and he opened his eyes. Marie must have felt the change, too, as she met his gaze. They focused on each other in the dark, then she pulled back with a swift gasp.

He couldn't begin to describe the disappointment that came over him.

Marie hadn't meant for the kiss to get so out of hand, but heavens above, it had. She pushed her way out of Charles's arms, and he released her at once. When she took another step away, desperate to create more distance between them, her leg pressed against the fountain, and her balance wavered just as before.

With a yelp, she reached out instinctively to grasp onto Charles again, knowing he could help her as he had the last time, but as he reached forward, both arms around her waist, he did not pull her safely back to firm footing.

Shock registered across his darkened features a moment before he lost his own balance, and together, they plummeted toward the frigid fountain water.

Marie drew in a frantic gasp, inhaling water as she landed hard against the bottom of the fountain, pain shooting through her right hip and shoulder. Charles fell in right after her, landing beside her as the knee-length water splashed around them both, covering them entirely as they scrambled to right themselves amidst the chaos.

She coughed and sputtered until she finally drew breath.

"Y-you hateful b-boy!" she stammered, prying her dress from her legs as she struggled to stand. "Now look what you've done!"

"What the devil did I do?" he blurted out. Water spewed from his lips and dripped from his dark hair to slide down the strong ridge of his nose. "You're the one who can't seem to stand upright."

"I was doing p-perfectly fine until you k-kissed me," she continued, the cold encompassing her as she coughed the water from her lungs.

He stared at her incredulously. "Until *I* kissed *you*? That fall must have rattled your brain entirely."

It wasn't the fall that had done so. But she wasn't about to admit that choosing to instigate the kiss between her and Charles Shepherd had been the best and worst decision of her life.

"You w-were begging for it," she said, very clearly grasping at straws.

He shook out his head, water flicking off his hair. "Was I?"

"Y-yes. How else am I to interpret your st-staring at me all night?"

He finally managed to stand, extending his hand to her, but she ignored it. She needed his help, but she wasn't about to touch him again. Not after how addle-brained she'd become at his kiss.

He grumbled incoherent words at her rejecting his help, then left the fountain first, water pouring off of his great figure like rushing falls.

Marie finally scrambled her way out of the water, as well, shivering as a draught of wind slid around her like an icy blanket.

She peered down at her sodden dress and slippers, knowing if her gown looked this worse for wear, the rest of her—hair and face included—were completely unpresentable.

"Well, now what do we do?" she questioned. "You've ruined my d-dress and a perfectly fine evening."

His eyes fixed on her as if he was attempting to decide if it was worth speaking or not. He glanced at the length of her, then shook his head and turned away.

"You should be grateful my parents raised me right," he grumbled, loosening his cravat and peeling his jacket off to reveal his shirt clinging to the ridges of his arms.

"What is that supposed to m-mean?" she questioned, her eyes lingering on his forearms as he rolled up his sleeves.

"You know what it means," he stated directly, draping the sopping jacket over his arm.

His eyes on her produced a heat within her that pushed aside the rest of her cold. "You are despicable."

She made to leave him there, uncomfortable with his attention and how it made her feel, but his hand reached out to stop her again.

She sighed with her eyes to the dark sky. "Will you please allow me to storm off just *once* this evening?"

"No," he stated matter-of-factly. "As your husband, it is my duty to see you are safely escorted wherever you may be. And as much as you love balls, I'm sure I am safe to assume that you have no intention of returning to the ballroom this evening."

She raised her chin. "None. Thanks to you."

"I will call for a carriage at the front of the house away from prying eyes. You may remain hidden in the shadows to maintain your dignity, then I shall escort you to the carriage and back to Grendale."

Marie hesitated, juggling between accepting his help and accepting public humiliation. "Fine."

"I appreciate the enthusiasm," he mumbled, then led the way through the hedges.

She fought off her pride trying to convince her to walk in the other direction and followed his broad shoulders swinging confidently back and forth.

She'd been clinging to those shoulders only minutes before.

"Is this how the rest of our marriage will look?" she questioned, desperate to find something to complain about. "You, exacting revenge if you don't get your way?"

He looked over his shoulder at her. "You needn't worry about what the rest of our marriage will look like. There may not be much more of a marriage to experience anyway."

He forged ahead, leaving Marie to walk two steps to his one as she attempted to keep up with him, though her thoughts were still back by the fountain, lingering on the kiss they'd shared—and the ominous foreboding he'd just delivered again.

The rest of the evening was unbearable. Charles attempted to offer Marie his hand as they entered the carriage in the quiet darkness, void of any prying eyes aside from the averted gazes of their family footman and groom.

True to form, Marie walked straight past Charles's extended fingers. She tripped on the step, grunted, then shoved his hand away as he tried to help her again.

"You really are that stubborn?" he asked.

"Yes."

When she finally entered the carriage, clambering across her wet skirts, Charles followed in after her, making a point to sit on the opposite side.

As the carriage rolled forward and the air between them filled with silence, Marie shivered, though he could see her desperate attempts to hide it. Her skirts still clung to her legs all the way to her thighs, and she attempted to unstick the fabric discreetly with her fingertips.

She must have been as aware as he was how translucent the material had become.

Reaching behind him, he pulled out the blanket Mother always brought along with her to late-night parties and balls, tossing it to the seat beside Marie.

"That is my mother's," he clarified. "I know you would not accept it if it were mine."

She glowered at him, then pulled the blanket across her body. He nearly sighed in relief at no longer having to fight his wayward eyes.

"How are your parents to get home if we take the carriage now?" she asked, eying the dark brown cover across her lap.

He'd already sent a footman to deliver the message to them both that he and Marie would be headed home early. No doubt Mother and Father would assume his return to Grendale with Marie was for one specific reason, but they would have a rude awakening when they discovered what exactly Charles had in mind for his future with Marie.

"Mr. Lloyd will return to the ball upon delivering us to Grendale," he replied.

She didn't respond, shivering once again, though this time with smaller movements.

She stared out of the window, and Charles took a moment to observe her in the dim light the carriage lantern outside allotted. Her skin was pale, her curls mere strings of black, and her shoulders were slightly slumped forward. But her lips were still curved in a lilting manner, and her eyebrows as dark and striking as ever.

The woman was stunning, even after all that had occurred tonight.

Another shiver racked her body, and a wave of guilt overcame him. "Sorry," he mumbled.

She turned toward him, her eyes condemning. "For what? Dragging me away from a perfectly fine ball and shouting at me? Or because you caused me to fall into the water? Or do you apologize for calling me lifeless and accusing me of mistreating your parents and orchestrating this marriage because I could not find a husband of my own?"

Charles winced. Laid out like that, he sounded rather like a cad. He supposed he *was* a cad. He also sounded mad now that he thought about it. What sort of woman would orchestrate all that had occurred today? Especially if what she'd said had been true— that he was the last man she'd ever wanted to marry.

She was far easier to hate when he thought her capable of such trickery. For when he thought of her as a woman in the same position as himself—forced by well-intentioned parents to give up the rest of their futures—she became far too relatable, and that made his guilt paramount.

He really had put his foot in his mouth far too many times today. Rowan, his Shakespeare-loving friend, would tell him to put forth more effort, or script some form of eloquent confession.

But that wasn't Charles.

"Can my apology be for all of that?" he asked.

She stared at him. "No."

He looked away with a frustrated sigh. He'd apologized thrice now, and still, Marie refused to accept his regret. Granted, his words had held a distinct defensive tone, but did he not receive credit for trying?

It was just as well she didn't forgive him, though. He hardly needed it with what he was planning for their future.

The rest of the journey home was met with silence, though Charles continued to monitor Marie's shivering until they pulled into Grendale Manor's drive.

He followed behind her in silence as they made their way to their bedchambers. Charles would have forgone following her feminine figure entirely by heading to the drawing room first, were he not desperate to change out of his own clothes.

When they reached their adjoining rooms—her door first— she stopped abruptly and spoke over her shoulder. "Goodnight, Mr. Shepherd."

Then she promptly entered her room and closed the door firmly behind her.

Charles shook his head with a scoff at her obvious rejection. Little did she know that the very idea of spending a moment longer with her would be akin to torture. Most of that was due to the fact that he could not extricate her kiss from his mind.

He strode to his room next, closing the door behind him, not waiting for his valet to strip off his sopping wet cravat and waistcoat.

He set them near the wardrobe just as the distinct sound of a lock echoed around his room. He eyed the door adjoined to Marie's, knowing full-well she'd secured the lock from her bedchamber on purpose.

Despite himself, Charles released a soft chuckle. He didn't think Marie believed that he would attempt to enter her room. Rather, he knew she'd locked the door on purpose—another way to say, *"I do not forgive you, Charles, and I never will."*

He shook his head and moved to stare out of the window,

eying the stars through the glass as he peeled off his shirtsleeves next.

He and Marie had been volatile today. There was no chance the two of them could survive a marriage together. They'd drive each other mad, and he had no desire to add "Be Sent to a Madhouse" on his list of adventures to accomplish this year.

Divorce wasn't an option—not without injuring Marie's reputation. And as much as he did not like the woman, he stood by his decision earlier. He would not harm her future.

After their conversation in the gardens that evening, however, with Marie's admission that she hadn't wanted to marry him either, it was obvious that something needed to be done.

He knew very little about annulments, but that had to be their clearest pathway forward. An annulment, time away from Society, and a proper bribe to her father would do the trick.

All he needed to do was convince his new bride—on their bridal tour, no less—to follow along with his plan.

He had little doubt that she would take any convincing at all. After all, she despised him as much as he despised her.

It was just a shame she kissed so well.

Chapter Eleven

M arie didn't sleep well that night, nor did she wish to wake up when she finally received rest that morning. She was roused from a deep slumber long after the sun had risen to a soft knocking upon her door. She ignored it for a moment, but when the sound persisted, she blinked as she looked around her, slightly disoriented until she caught sight of the stockings draped over a nearby chair.

They were nearly dry after her night in the fountain with her husband—something that sounded far more romantic than it actually had been. Especially considering said husband sounded very much like he was attempting to end their marriage prematurely.

"Ma'am?"

The soft voice came from the door after another knock, and finally, Marie extracted herself from her bed to answer.

"My apologies, Jane," Marie said as she allowed her lady's maid into the room. "I forgot I locked my door last night after you'd left."

She'd done so loud enough for Charles to hear again—or so she hoped.

"Not to worry, ma'am," Jane replied. "I'm sorry to wake you, but we're scheduled to leave in just under an hour. Mr. Charles Shepherd has requested an eleven o'clock departure."

Marie sighed. There she was again, being dictated by the man. Unless...

A slow smile spread across her lips, and without a word, she scribbled a note to Charles.

My dearest husband,

I understand that you would like to depart at eleven o'clock. I regret to inform you that I shall need at least a few hours more to prepare for our journey.

You see, I did not sleep very well last night and am quite afraid I am coming down with a cold due to the occurrences of the evening. In fact, we may need to request the presence of a doctor here to ensure I am well. A professional opinion is always best, as you well know.

At any rate, physician or not, I cannot see myself being able to leave until two o'clock at the earliest.

I do apologize for the inconvenience this may cause. But you understand.

Yours,
Marie

There. That should buy her an hour or two.

Marie folded the correspondence, then beckoned Jane to deliver it, all the while smiling to herself at the knowledge of how the letter would be received.

After breakfast, which she took in her room, and a very slow start to the morning, reading a few chapters of her latest book she had never before been interested in and brushing her hair at least a few hundred times—which she had also never done before—Marie finally felt motivated enough to dress, so she called for Jane to return to her chambers.

Jane came and brought with her Charles's response.

To my perfect wife,

How terribly sorry I am to hear that you have caught cold after your antics last evening. Although, I must say, that does not surprise me, what with your obviously weak constitution.

That being said, two o'clock will suit my schedule perfectly. As thrilled as I am at the prospect of spending the next fortnight with you, I am more than happy to wait until you are well enough to travel. In fact, why do we not push the time even further? What would you say to postponing the bridal tour indefinitely?

My mother will wonder, of course, at our hesitance to proceed with the tour, but I suppose she will overcome whatever disappointment she may feel.

As for calling for a physician, I'd hate to worry my mother unnecessarily. Perhaps we ought to wait to see if you will be miraculously healed of your ailments on your own.

Do keep me updated.

Your anxious husband,
Charles

Marie frowned. It was almost as if he'd expected her to push back on their departure time. Did he already know her so well? Well, he wouldn't expect what she had to say next.

To my charming husband,

Your thoughtfulness knows no bounds—and your ability to manifest the future. As it so happens, I have been miraculously healed and will be ready to leave within an hour. I would not wish to make you wait a moment longer without me.

I know how much you love our time together.

Do tell your mother of our plan to still leave. If she wishes to know why there has been back-and-forth, perhaps you might simply explain what you did last night. She will understand perfectly then, I am certain.

Your Just-As-Equally-Thoughtful Wife,
Marie

PS. Have you any requests as to which personality you would prefer for the trip and fortnight ahead? I am happy to assume whichever you prefer. Although, I do promise to not behave like a handkerchief again. Unless, of course, you are in need of me when you sneeze.

With another satisfied smile, she bade Jane once more to deliver the note, then awaited her return.

Over the next half hour, the two of them worked together to ensure Marie was dressed and ready for their departure. With two minutes to spare, she left her room behind, only to find Mrs. Shepherd walking toward her down the otherwise empty corridor.

"I came to deliver this," Mrs. Shepherd said with a warm smile. "It is from my son. No doubt a love note of some sort."

Marie *highly* doubted that was what the letter held, still she accepted it with a smile.

They moved down the corridor together. Half a dozen portraits decorated the walls, each filled with various paintings of horses, dogs, and hunting parties.

"How are you faring, my dear?" Mrs. Shepherd asked. "We missed your presence throughout the rest of the ball last night, but I gather it was for good reason?"

Marie could hardly crush her spirits. "Your son and I had a very interesting...conversation."

Mrs. Shepherd's features fell, but she hid them swiftly with a smile. "Well, I do hope you enjoy yourselves over the coming weeks. My bridal tour with Mr. Shepherd was the best thing for our marriage. And...do be patient with Charles. I know he can be quite a difficult person to be around at times, but once a person breaks down his rather crusted exterior, there is no one who will love you more fully."

Marie nodded, unable to even concoct a word.

Mrs. Shepherd was putting far too much stock in her son's abilities to be a good person.

"I will meet you downstairs," Mrs. Shepherd said. "I must fetch Mr. Shepherd's walking stick."

Marie nodded, waiting until Mrs. Shepherd was out of sight before ripping open the burning letter in her hands.

Dearest Darling Marie,

Thank you for the opportunity to choose my own wife for the day. I believe I have seen enough of each and would prefer now to witness the amiable woman I was promised by my mother from the beginning—as I have yet to see her.

Your Patient Husband,

Charles

PS. I, myself, shall remain as I have always been—honor-able, respectful, and ever-doting.

Marie scoffed in disgust, shaking her head and tearing the paper in two before sliding the pieces into her reticule. No wonder he'd delivered it at the last moment. He must have known it would allow him to get the final word in.

She had a mind to show the correspondence to Mrs. Shepherd. Charles would be sure to receive the scolding of the century. But she didn't wish for the woman to worry any further about Marie's relationship with Charles. At any rate, there was no guarantee Mrs. Shepherd would recognize the satire within their letters anyway. She certainly hadn't before.

Marie hadn't either, but now that she knew the man, his personality was obvious. He couldn't be counted on for seriousness to any degree.

She arrived in the entryway a moment later, walking toward the open doorway. Her thoughts were preoccupied with how to respond to Charles when his voice drifted toward her from where the two carriages lined the drive.

He spoke with another man who boasted a large mustache and thin build, the two of them appearing deep in conversation. She could not catch a word, their heads slightly ducked in a conspiratorial manner.

The gentleman caught her eye first, and he straightened. Charles glanced over his shoulder and smiled with a self-satisfied air, then turned back to the gentleman with a single nod.

The gentleman departed, and Charles faced her.

Marie narrowed her eyes at his impassive expression. His words from the night before slid into her memory.

"There may not be much more of a marriage to experience anyway."

She hadn't the faintest notion how he would obtain a divorce or an annulment, but she would not put such an action past someone like Childish Charlie—a man who would clearly stop at nothing to get his own way.

His parents certainly wouldn't be happy. Father would be livid. And Marie? Marie would be ruined, but at least she would not be forced to be with someone who loathed her.

"There you are," Charles said as she walked down the steps toward him and the already-loaded carriages. "I see you are feeling better."

"Your palpable concern has appeared to revive me."

Before another word could be shared, the Shepherds appeared behind her, and goodbyes were exchanged. Shortly after, Marie and Charles were escorted off the premises in their carriage—the help following behind in a coach of their own.

Charles didn't speak across from her, and the pleasant expression on his features did nothing to settle her nerves, nor did his constant fidgeting. He tapped his fingers against his leg and persistently shifted in his seat.

After the thirteenth time of Charles tapping out some absentminded tune, Marie couldn't bear it any longer. She turned to face him directly with a pointed look.

"Do you *ever* hold still?"

He finally settled, his jawline highlighted as it poked out from his high collar and cravat. "Is my movement upsetting you?"

"It is rather distracting, that is all."

"My apologies. I would never wish to upset my *wife*."

He smirked at the word, then instantly resumed his movements. This time, he bounced his leg up and down so greatly, he proved to rattle the carriage more fully than the bumpy road beneath them.

She stifled a sigh, ignoring him for as long as possible before catching his growing smile.

"You appear more at ease this morning," she said.

"I am."

"Why is that?"

He turned to face her, and Marie's breath slipped from her lips. She had never seen Charles with an actual pleasant expression across his features. His eyes were as dark as hers with hair perhaps even darker, but there was a lightness to his features—brows tipped slightly up in the center, smile lines near the edges of his eyes—that made him appear far less intimidating than he had been.

"I smile," he began, "because I have finally decided to find a way out of our current...predicament."

Her stomach tightened. "Predicament? You refer to our marriage, I assume."

"If you wish to call it that."

So Marie hadn't been imagining matters. Charles truly was scheming to end their marriage prematurely.

He resembled his twin a great deal here with that self-satisfied smile. She hadn't seen much of Tristan. Only a brief introduction once. Still, she'd recognized the difference in the brothers immediately. Charles's eyebrows were just a degree farther apart, and his smile broader. More than that, his lack of awareness and devil-may-care attitude practically leapt from his person.

Which was why it rankled her to no end to admit how greatly she enjoyed kissing him last night.

"Who was that man you were speaking with earlier?" she asked.

"Our steward, Mr. Page. I have sworn him to secrecy and subsequently tasked him with learning more about what constitutes grounds for an annulment."

She stared. "For...us."

"Well, yes. You told me yourself last night you were forced into this arrangement as much as I was." He paused. "Unless of course, you were lying..."

She narrowed her eyes. "I was not lying. I *was* persuaded to accept this marriage."

"There you have it. I am not well-versed in how to obtain an annulment—"

"Shocking," she interrupted.

"However, I believe we may be able to obtain one on the grounds of being forced to wed."

That unsettling feeling continued to creep up behind Marie, a lurking dread of having no future.

"Unless I am mistaken, no pistol was leveled at us to force us to agree to the union," she said.

He looked away with a shrug. "There may not have been a pistol, but threats were fired clear enough. At any rate, Mr. Page will inform us the moment he learns anything new so that we might both escape this marriage we have no desire to continue."

He said nothing further, merely tapped his boots against the carriage floor in a rhythmic pattern, appearing perfectly content.

Marie, however, was not. She wasn't pleased with the husband she'd married, but her future had finally been secured. Now, all thought of leading a somewhat peaceful existence—at least in being financially cared for—vanished.

"You do want the marriage to end, do you not?" Charles asked.

"I..."

She couldn't answer. *Did* she wish for that security to end? To return to her family and live with a disappointed father and absent-minded mother? She didn't think she could bear the whispers that would spread about her spinsterhood and inability to keep a husband even *after* marriage.

"Marie?" Charles pressed, his brow low.

She needed to explain her hesitance before he assumed something ridiculous—like that she'd miraculously fallen for him.

"I would prefer having a marriage with a man who loved me as much as I loved him." She spoke the truth, even if she no longer believed love was in her future. "However, I must admit, I do not see how a life after an annulment would be worth living. Particularly for myself as a woman."

"You refer to your reputation."

She nodded in silence.

He didn't speak for a moment, seeming to gather his thoughts. Finally, he leaned forward in his seat across from her, resting his arms on his knees as he laced his fingers together. They were only a few inches away from her own legs, so she scooted farther back in the carriage seat, allotting herself more room in preparation of any wayward bump from the carriage.

"You have every right to be concerned," he said softly. "but I meant what I said before. I will not proceed if there is a chance that your reputation might be damaged."

The look in his eyes was unlike anything Marie had seen within them—something akin to sincerity. Her heart fought back against his words, but they slipped beneath her defenses, and for some reason she could not fathom, an emotion rose within her at his intent to protect her.

But Oakleys did not cry.

His eyes lingered a moment too long on her, so she shifted in her seat and averted her gaze.

"When do you expect a response from Mr. Page?" she asked, smoothing out her skirts and staring at his fingers still just out of reach from her legs. "And what of my father? Your parents? How will you assuage them?"

"I have yet to solve those conundrums," he said. "Perhaps we may work together on that?"

Work together as husband and wife to no longer *be* husband and wife? She'd never heard of anything so preposterous. Still, she agreed, if only to prevent him from assuming she wished to be married to him still.

That would be more humiliating than anything.

"So, we are in agreement?" he asked.

The carriage jostled above a dip in the road, and just as she'd expected, his fingers brushed against her knee. The touch was so faint, she wasn't entirely sure *he'd* felt it, as he remained leaning forward.

"Yes," she breathed. "We are in agreement."

"Very well. Then we shall continue forward unless the path

affects either of us negatively. Or, of course, in the circumstance that you change your mind and wish to remain married to me after all—in which case, I will perform my duty and remain your husband. Agreed?"

Marie stiffened, the flood of warmth emptying her person in great waves. She'd been swept up with his promises of security until that last caveat.

"Unless I change my mind and wish to remain married to you," she repeated.

"Yes."

She raised her chin. "And unless *you* change *your* mind and wish to remain married to *me*."

A smirk of disbelief lifted the corners of his lips, and he finally straightened, leaning back against the seat in a relaxed manner. "Of course."

Her pride flared, sizzling from her person like steam from a teapot. "Is that so very farfetched?"

"Not at all."

His smooth voice and level-headed responses were really beginning to irk her.

"Well, worry not"—she added *Childish Charlie* to her own thoughts—"I will *not* change my mind."

Nor would she ever. A marriage with Charles Shepherd sounded worse than purgatory.

She straightened in her seat and pulled her gaze to the window. "Do keep me updated the moment you receive word from Mr. Page. I am *quite* interested in his solutions."

"As am I," Charles said, apparently not catching on to her clear desire to be finished speaking with him—forever if luck would have it. "But we must prepare ourselves if our only solution is to remain wedded."

She pulled on a face as if she'd just smelled rotting cabbage. "As I said, do keep me updated."

She shifted her body away from him, and this time, Charles accepted the hint.

They fell silent, and Marie was left to her own thoughts.

She had very little hope that whatever Mr. Page found out about annulments, her reputation would be left unscathed. She also doubted that the knowledge would prevent Charles from seeking an annulment anyway. If he could not keep a vow made before God, why would he keep a mere promise to Marie?

Whatever happened, she knew one thing. She would die before allowing Charles to discover that she would rather remain in their marriage than leave it.

Chapter Twelve

Hours later, the carriage pulled to a stop before the smallest cottage Charles had ever laid eyes on.

"Woewood Cottage?" Marie asked, her eyes moving across the two-storied house. *"This* is where we are staying?"

"Are you surprised? Of course this is where they wish us to spend the next fortnight together." He lowered his breath, mumbling to himself. "We hardly have the space to breathe our own air here."

With off-white bricks and a roof in shambles, the edifice had clearly seen better days, though the small, white door and red-bordered windows lent a certain charm to the overall feel. Pink and red rose bushes with their early blooms shone brightly in front of the two lower windows, and strands of ivy crawled to the three windows on the second floor.

There could not be much of a dining area with such limited space, nor could there be above three or four rooms—which Charles knew was precisely the point. Instead of sending them on an actual bridal tour visiting relatives and viewing beautiful locations throughout England, their parents had chosen to send him and Marie to the smallest home in the country—no doubt another attempt to solidify their union.

Mother and Father were never subtle. It was a wonder Charles and Tristan had turned out so well.

Charles followed Marie as they took themselves on a tour through the house, which was even smaller than it had appeared on the outside.

With rooms that flowed into one another, the cottage's layout was fairly standard—though the dining area only had room for four seatings and the sitting room barely had space for three chairs.

"It is quite small," Marie said in a soft voice as they peeked into the kitchen on the main level of the house. "But at least it is clean."

Charles eyed the corridor walls draped with spare webs at the edges. "Depends on your definition of *clean*."

"Frightened of spiders, are you?" she asked over her shoulder. "Worry not. I am no stranger to trapping them for my mother. I'd be happy to provide my delicate husband with the same courtesy."

"That won't be necessary, but thank you all the same for your generous offer."

Charles could handle a little spider now and again, but the worst of the matter was when they climbed the stairs—stairs that were barely wide enough to fit one person at a time—and reached the bedchambers.

Each door was closed apart from the first room at the start of the corridor. Together, they made their way toward it, both of them leaning halfway into the room and peering at the two trunks resting side by side near the bed.

His and Marie's trunks...placed in the same room. No doubt this was another request from Mother.

In the same moment he glanced at Marie, she glanced at him, and her expression said it all.

She did not approve.

He didn't pay too much attention to her expression, however, for the small doorframe they stood within brought them nearly as close to each other as the fountain had. Their eyes dropped to each other's mouths simultaneously, but Marie looked away first.

"One room will not do," she said. "Especially if we are to seek an annulment."

He watched her in silence.

She must have taken his lack of response as confusion rather than what it was—a desperate attempt to stop himself from replaying their kiss in his mind over and over again.

"Correct me if I am mistaken," she began, "but I was under the impression that for a couple to seek an annulment, they must remain...apart."

"I believe you are correct," he said softly.

Energy sparked between them as their eyes met again, and Charles's breathing shallowed.

"Will that be too difficult for you?" she asked.

He barely registered her words. All he could think about was having just one more look at her lips. That was all he needed. One look, and he'd be satiated.

And yet, when he glanced again at those perfect, rosy lips and traced the gentle slopes and curves with his eyes, he knew in that moment, his desire for her would never be quenched until he could drink from those lips again.

"Charles," she repeated sternly, "will that be too difficult for you?"

"Not for me," he lied. "You?"

"Not a chance."

A smile tugged at his lips. "Are you certain? You are the one who kissed *me* if you recall."

Her eyes flicked between his, then finally, she looked away. "I assure you, that was a moment of weakness and fury that will not be repeated. At any rate, I think it wise if we do not share a room" —she motioned to the small bed barely suitable for one person— "or *that*."

He entered the room, pushing aside images of holding Marie

in his arms as they fell asleep together. It would be necessary to hold her, after all, in so small a bed.

"I'll have mine moved directly." He glanced to the wardrobe. "And the clothing of mine they have no doubt placed within there, as well. I only hope they've already prepared another room."

"I can check for spiders first, if you'd feel safer."

He rang the servant's bell near the bed, then turned to face her. She remained in the doorway, her eyes upon him with an expression comparable to when they'd first met—calculating but otherwise entirely imperceptible.

Was she uncomfortable with him standing in her room? That had to be it. She'd agreed to the annulment, after all. Her desire for their relationship to remain platonic was obvious. Charles, of course, was willing to oblige, despite his level of attraction to her. He'd meant what he'd said before. He wouldn't do anything to injure her.

A fleeting thought flickered through his mind. If he followed through with the annulment, would he be back in the running for losing the bet? Or was his marriage, short as it was, enough to secure a win? He was fine either way, but he knew alerting his friends of any marriage would put them into a frenzy.

Perhaps Charles would pull a page out of Mother's book and do a little matchmaking himself, then. Thomas and Andrew might already be married, and Rowan was promised to another. But Ambrose Hartley—good, ole, overplanning Rosie—might find Marie humorous. Perhaps even sullen Leonard would enjoy her company.

And yet, the mere thought of Marie being wrapped in the arms of any of his school friends, sharing her kisses with them and bestowing warm smiles upon them, filled his stomach with that same jealous frustration that had encompassed him at the ball.

"I ought to be out of here soon enough," he reassured her— and himself—as he moved to stand beside his trunk.

She made no response, her petite figure remaining resolutely in the doorframe. Her form and posture were always flawless, but in her dark blue traveling clothes, she was regality itself. A few dark curls had come loose during their carriage ride and now trailed down one of her shoulders. He fought the urge to close the distance between them to see if the strands were as smooth as they appeared.

An awkward silence filled the space between them, and the absence of any servant's footsteps became more and more obvious.

"Does the bell not work?" she asked, motioning to the strip of fabric draped near the wall.

He tried again, but after no response, he sighed. Marie obviously wished for him to leave the intimacy of her room and would not relax until he did so. But who knew how long they'd be waiting?

"I'll just take care of it myself," he muttered, moving to the trunks again as he removed his jacket and rolled up his shirtsleeves.

Finally, he hoisted his trunk onto his shoulder, then made to leave the room, but Marie was still standing in the doorway, her eyes on his forearms.

For the first time since he'd met her, he could read her expression. Clear as the skies that morning, approval and admiration shone in her eyes as she watched him handle the trunk.

His chest opened, and his shoulders straightened of their own accord. That same feeling that stirred within him during their kiss returned, and suddenly, the weight of the trunk was insignificant.

These sorts of feelings were not entirely unexpected—after all, he'd already admitted to finding Marie attractive. But if they were to seek an annulment, if he was truly wishing to end their union, he certainly shouldn't be dwelling on them...*or* wishing for more.

"Pardon," he said, motioning to the door.

She blinked once, then stepped aside with reddened cheeks.

All Charles could do was hide his smile as he left the room.

Marie, once again, did not sleep well that night, or the night after that. This was, in part, due to the flimsy nature of her bed, as she feared one sudden roll might render her flat on the floor.

What made matters worse, however, were the veritably paper-thin walls within the cottage.

Charles had found the room next to Marie's prepared, so he'd settled there, but with every movement he made, she could hear his footsteps, the whining of the chair near his desk, and the creaking of his bed. She never heard voices, however, only his movements, but it made matters very difficult to *not* imagine him pacing about his room, dressing for bed, and climbing beneath his covers.

Their first full day at Woewood, she only left her room to join him for church. The two of them slipped in at the back, then left before a word could be spoken to either of them. When they returned, Marie retreated directly to her room, and there she remained for the entirety of the day, not having the energy or desire to deal with her husband—or the constant reminder of how attracted to him she was.

After sunrise on the second day, she heard him roll out of his bed and watched him leave the cottage on what she could only assume was a morning walk. Hoping to eat without him and anxious for a view beyond her four walls, she dressed and slipped from her room to take her breakfast downstairs at a leisurely pace.

She didn't need to rush. Charles would remain out of doors for as long as possible, no doubt attempting to rid himself of his seemingly endless energy by bounding across fields like a young buck or scaling trees like a feral tomcat.

However, as she scooped a generous helping of apricot preserve onto her piece of toast and brought it to her mouth, Charles walked into the kitchen.

With the toast just before her lips and her mouth hanging open, she froze. She had never seen a person less prepared for breakfast than Charles as he entered the dining area. Father had always dressed appropriately, fully clothed and ready to eat. But not Charles. He wore no cravat nor jacket, and his waistcoat was fully unbuttoned, hanging open to reveal his flowing, white shirt that hung open at the top.

Truthfully, she should have expected nothing less than complete indecorum from the man.

Anyway, what was he doing home so early? She would have thought he'd have taken a much longer walk.

"Morning," he said casually, pulling out a seat across from her and helping himself to his own toast and poached egg.

Marie still stared. The ridges in his forearm shifted as he reached for the preserves she'd just used but had yet to enjoy. He took a bite, chewed it heartily, then swallowed. She stared at his throat bobbing up and down, then her eyes trailed down to the curves of his chest.

Charles remained entirely unaware of her stares until he reached for his teacup and paused. He glanced over his shoulder, then back at her. "Something the matter?"

She averted her gaze with a raised chin. "I am unaccustomed to eating breakfast with someone in such a state of undress, that is all."

He peered down at his open shirt as if unaware of what he wore until that moment. "My apologies. I grew rather overheated on a quick walk this morning and forgot to button again."

She stared hard at her toast, then finally managed a bite. The apricots weren't as satisfying as she'd hoped. Not when all she wanted to do was stare longer at Charles's gaping shirt.

Her eyes flicked back to him, trailing down the ridges of his neck.

"I will change if you wish me to," he said through chews of his toast. "Seeing as how I appear to be distracting you."

A spark of humor glinted in his eyes, but she refused to be embarrassed, standing from the table. "There is no need. I am finished anyway."

He eyed her full plate. "Returning to your room?"

Marie paused at the door. "I was considering it."

"I suppose I won't see you again until morning."

Did he miss her? Had he felt as lonely as Marie had? If their marriage was to be annulled, she didn't wish to grow accustomed to seeing him, but perhaps...

"Well, enjoy your time wallowing away." He paused, then added with an apparent glint in his eye, "and skulking at me from your window."

Marie had obviously gone mad. Why else would she have ever thought that Charles would miss her, other than to torment her?

"I may as well remain in my bedchamber," she stated pointedly. "After all, there is nothing out here worthy to capture my attention."

He smiled amusedly, taking a final bite of his toast and chewing in all of his undressed-glory.

"What are *you* to do this morning?" she asked. "Bound about the grounds like a directionless pup?"

He leaned back in his seat, lazily propping his elbow against the back of it. "I think I will, actually. Or perhaps I'll make the short walk to the village to see if Mr. Page has written. You're welcome to join me if you'd like. Although, the distance might be a bit strenuous for you. It may last longer than an *entire* five minutes."

This repartee had to stop at some point, did it not? One of them had to be the bigger person. One of them had to apologize, forgive, and start afresh.

Unfortunately, her pride was louder than her moral compass, so ending their arguments would not begin with her.

"That is a generous offer," she returned. "However, I do think I ought to remain indoors. It is better for one's complexion." She eyed his skin up and down and wrinkled her nose. "Though I take it you care about no such thing."

In truth, while Charles's skin was a few shades tanner than most dandies, Marie couldn't deny that she preferred it. The color gave him a healthy glow—as if the sun had been unable to resist kissing Charles, too.

"You know," he said with a smile, "I quite like you, Marie. Your little slights and quirks are more enjoyable, now that I know I won't be required to manage them for the rest of my days."

"That's interesting. I was just now thinking the very same about your entire personality."

He smirked, clearly amused with her comments. He stood from the table, and she raised her chin to maintain his gaze.

"So you'll not be joining me in the village, then?" he asked.

"No. I think it will be best if we remain apart as much as possible until Mr. Page writes with news."

"Afraid to fall in love with me, are you?"

She let out a forced laugh. "That is the least of my concerns, Mr. Shepherd."

"And what is your greatest?"

She leaned toward him with a sickly-sweet smile. "That I will strangle you before I get the chance to annul our marriage."

He threw back his head, his throat fully visible as it bobbed up and down with his genuine laugh.

Marie turned away, walking from the room as he ended his laughter with a happy sigh.

Marie should have been sullen and offended, but instead, she found herself unable to wipe the smile from her own lips.

Arguing with Charles was becoming more and more enjoyable, and that alone was cause enough for concern.

Chapter Thirteen

The next afternoon, Charles walked away from the post office in Orpington, once again empty-handed as he crossed the cobbled streets and headed back in the direction of Woewood Cottage.

It was far too early to expect a correspondence from Mr. Page anyway, but Charles had managed to send off his letter to Tristan, despite Mother's desire to keep his brother in the dark.

Tristan,

I'm sorry to begin this letter with terrible news, but our hunting trip must be postponed indefinitely, as I am presently occupied with my new wife. I'm certain you read that word again just to be sure, so let me settle your astonishment by confirming that I am, indeed, married.

If you have any questions, ask Mother. I'm certain she will be more than happy to fill you in on all the details, though she may or may not be honest with you. As such, you may already have a guess as to how this union came about, especially when you discover that my wife is the one and only

Marie Oakley. You will remember her as the woman Mother has tried to force upon me for the last year.

All I shall say presently is that Mother was doing what Mother does best—meddling. At any rate, I have reason to suspect that circumstances between me and my new bride will change soon enough, so worry yourself not with the details.

I will explain all when we next see one another, though I have no notion as to when that will be. I do hope London is treating you well. Give Thomas, Andrew, Ambrose, and Leonard my best. Though might I suggest not telling them about my marriage quite yet? I should hate to worry the rest of you unattached gentlemen needlessly concerning the bet if this is all going to come to an end anyway. Unless an ended marriage still counts toward the wager.

That being said, I do hope you are spending plenty of time in finding a wife. If this farce does proceed, three of us will be out of the running. Do try not to waste your money needlessly. You may rest assured that if you are not actively searching for a bride, Mother may already be plotting.

Charles

Despite his parents' wishes, Charles had never been one to keep secrets from Tristan, so he had no remorse whatsoever in informing his brother as to what had occurred.

Charles had, however, stopped himself from sending off the letter he'd written to Mother—in which he'd laid out his plans to annul his marriage with Marie. Delivering the news in a correspondence seemed rather cowardly, though, so he had tucked the letter away instead, deciding to speak with her in person just as soon as Mr. Page provided him a way forward.

If Mr. Page provided him a way forward.

Bracing himself for that familiar tightening of his chest that always came at the thought of remaining married, Charles furrowed his brow when, to his great surprise, that tightness did not appear.

Instead, the image of Marie watching him carry his trunk flickered in his mind's eye, and the approval he'd seen caused his heart to trip.

The reaction was concerning, to say the least. Was he actually developing an attraction toward the woman? An attraction that stretched beyond physicality? He'd said himself he was beginning to find her enjoyable. Was that why he'd known a degree of disappointment when she'd refused to join him in the village?

This would certainly put a damper on his attempt to seek an annulment—falling for the woman he was determined to no longer be with. Or worse, falling for the woman who no longer wished to be with him.

His thoughts continued whizzing busily about his mind as he left the village behind and walked along the lane that led back to the cottage.

He tipped his hat to a few ladies headed in the opposite direction, their eyes lingering on him a moment longer than necessary before they whispered and giggled quietly to one another the moment he passed.

Typically, Charles enjoyed the boost of confidence such looks gave him, but this time, his mind remained on Marie. Would she have noticed the girls staring? Would she have become jealous as he had when she'd danced with half the men at the ball?

No, she would feel no such thing because she wanted out of this marriage.

Just as he did.

He was still upset about not being able to choose his own future. He simply needed the reminder.

Creating a mental list, he rehearsed his grievances against her, and yet, his mind continuously rebutted each item he'd once complained about.

Her shifting personality had been due to her fear of rejection. Her lifeless behavior had entirely vanished. And her staunch propriety had been thrown promptly out the window when she'd kissed him in the gardens at night.

The only one that stood firm, however, was her lack of adventurous spirit. She remained in her room yesterday after breakfast —just as he'd guessed—and he had yet to see her today. What did she do in there all day besides dwell in her own thoughts? Being with someone like that would cause Charles to lose his mind before long.

Then again, knowing Marie, she might *encourage* him to leave. She was fiercely independent, after all, having yet to even accept his hand upon entering a carriage.

This was another reason he and Marie did not suit. Charles had always received a great deal of value in the knowledge that he was needed, whether that was by Tristan when they were children in fistfights against larger, older boys, or when their friends had needed a laugh or a simple distraction to help calm them during their tour around Europe.

He'd seen Andrew Langford's wife, Sophie, rely on her husband to keep her reputation safe. Mother depended on Father to keep her entertained and cared for. With no wife to aid in such a way, no wife to *need* him in such a way, what value could Charles ever provide to his own marriage?

His footsteps slowed, weighed down by his heavy thoughts as he passed by the lych gate of the local church. He glanced through the small, roofed archway, spotting the stone chapel a good distance from it and a bench that was occupied by a woman.

He looked away, only to return a moment later as he recognized Marie. She wore a light blue pelisse that matched the ribbons in her hair, and her straw bonnet rested on her lap. She sat turned away from Charles's view until she straightened, and her tear-strewn cheeks glinted in the light.

Charles stiffened. He had never seen Marie exude any such emotion before. He might have even thought her *incapable* of crying. And yet, as she reached up with gloveless hands to dab at her tears with a wrinkled handkerchief, the evidence was undeniable. And he had no idea what to do about it.

Obviously, she had never revealed this side of her before because she did not trust Charles. How could she when all he'd done was complain about their marriage for three days? Was that why she'd become emotional? Or were these tears residual from the cruelty he'd shown her before?

He shifted his boots uncomfortably in the dirt, still unnoticed by Marie as he remained hidden behind the covered gate. Crying women always made him question himself. He never knew what to say or what to do. This was, in part, due to Mother, for her tears could always be turned on and off with the blink of an eye.

But Marie seemed genuinely upset. What could he do for her if she did not want his help? He would no doubt make matters worse whatever his efforts were.

And yet, as she swiped away another tear, his heart twisted. He had to help her. He *yearned* to help her. For not only was he her husband, he was also the cause of her tears.

Marie tried to stop, but her tears slipped down her cheeks with no inclination to cease. It was as if her body knew she was free to release years of pent-up emotion, for not only was she away from Father, but she was also away from Charles, who, she suspected, despised tears as much as Father did.

That was precisely why she'd walked to the church. With the cottage's thin walls, she'd have no chance at privacy.

Still, she didn't approve of the emotion either, and soon, instead of dabbing at her tears, she swiped the moisture away in frustration with her bare hands. She hated crying. It prevented her stoic front from protecting her vulnerable state. And yet, she could not help herself.

She'd been fine for two days now, but being alone once again, her thoughts shifted to sorrow as she realized that her loneliness was going to increase tenfold if her marriage with Charles continued *or* ended.

If it continued, they would remain in this manner their entire lives—him leaving, her staying. And if it ended, she would be without a husband forever.

Logically, she knew he would not annul the marriage if her reputation was at risk, but he seemed so determined, she feared he would stop at nothing to seize control of his future. Which would leave her with no future at all.

A fresh bout of tears streamed from her eyes, and once again, she aggressively swiped at them. Thank heavens Charles could not see her. If he did, he would—

"Marie?"

She gasped, swinging around on the bench to find Charles himself approaching her with hesitant footsteps.

"Charles," she said, clearing her throat and turning away for a brief moment to wipe whatever moisture remained on her face. The shock from his sudden appearance finally put a stopper on her tears. "Enjoying your walk?"

He stopped a few paces away from her. "I am. I was walking by the church when I...saw you."

Blast. He'd seen her crying in all her state, then. She drew a settling breath. "Yes, I wished to enjoy a small walk."

He was silent for a moment. "I thought you didn't like being out of doors."

"I never said that," she stated. "I merely said I *prefer* to be indoors."

Although, now that she thought about it, perhaps that was because Mother and Father preferred to be indoors—and she simply did not wish to be alone when she ventured outside. They always complained about the heat or the rain or the sunshine or the clouds, when in reality, Marie might not have minded being out of doors if she was with someone who enjoyed it. Like Charles.

"May I sit with you for a moment?" he asked, still standing a few steps away.

"If you wish."

He sat down beside her, the wood creaking as he settled a foot's length away. Silence fell when he removed his hat and circled the rim around his hands.

She had assumed he'd immediately pelt her with questions as to why she was walking alone or why she was crying, but as each moment ticked by in continued silence, her worries quieted.

He must not have wanted to speak as much as she didn't want to.

They both stared across the small field that extended off the grounds of the church. Tall grass rippled in the gentle wind that brought with it the scent of the hyacinths growing in the nearby woods. Blue skies appeared between thick clouds, and all was quiet apart from the subtle bleating of distant sheep and the rustling of leaves from the oak tree they sat beneath.

Her desire to weep had vanished, and finally, she sat in serene peace—the one only discoverable after a healing cry. The one only experienced when being near the calm and steady presence of another.

Never would she have guessed that Charles would be that person for her.

She glanced over at him, his own peace soothing every inch of his expression—brow soft, lips loosely parted, and more apparent than anything, a still body.

Marie had never known him to be so tranquil. Was he doing this for her? She did not wish for him to feel obligated to do so.

"You needn't—" she began.

"I have some things—" he started at the same moment.

Their eyes met, and a small smile passed between them.

Instead of intense sparks of anger or attraction that typically accompanied their conversations, a serenity filled the space.

Charles motioned with a tip of his head for her to take the lead.

Marie nodded. "I was only going to say that you needn't remain here if you wish to continue with your walk. I know you do not care to sit still for long periods of time."

He paused. "I don't recall ever telling you that."

"You didn't. But you are almost always on the move, whether you're walking or standing." Her lips curved. "Or sitting. I also noticed that you appeared more horrified to discover that I didn't do much out of doors than when you discovered that you were going to have to marry me."

His shoulders lifted as he gave a little laugh. "Mr. Berryman and my parents always scolded me for not being able to hold still as a child. I thought I had gotten better from my youth, but I suppose I am not as inconspicuous as I had hoped."

"No, you are not." Their eyes caught. "What was it *you* were about to say?"

His eyes lingered on hers, and he appeared as if he was in a different world for a moment before he blinked and looked away. "I was going to say that I have a few things I wished to apologize for."

Chapter Fourteen

That was the last thing Marie had expected.

"Oh," she replied.

"I saw you crying," he continued. "I should like to help you, but I don't wish to impose."

Her parents had always avoided her when she'd cried as a child, though they'd done their best to comfort her with a brief pat to the top of her head. She'd soon learned that it was far easier to *not* cry than to expect anything more. It was just as well. She still loved her parents, even if she longed for more compassion from them.

"Am I?" he asked when she didn't respond. "Imposing, I mean."

"No, you are not."

He nodded, swallowing hard. "Then I shall continue by apologizing first for my behavior—from the time of our first meeting to my slights yesterday morning. And especially for when I spoke those horrible words to my parents."

Marie shifted uncomfortably on the bench. She wasn't certain she'd ever received an apology from anyone before. She didn't know what to make of it.

"You've already apologized for your words, Charles."

He scoffed, raking his fingers through his hair. "I did nothing but make excuses for myself. I have allowed the circumstances surrounding our connection to cloud my judgement and have behaved despicably because of it. I never should have..." His words trailed off, and he shook his head, a deep line etched in his brow as he watched her. "I never should have said those words about you. Not only were they unkind, but they were entirely untrue. I have consistently blamed you and accused you of all manner of falsehoods. I cannot tell you how much I regret my childish actions. I am truly sorry, Marie, for everything."

A weight began to lift from around her, and an airy feeling took flight in her chest. She'd never felt so carefree...so *cared for*.

"I understand if you cannot forgive me, but I—"

"I do forgive you."

He eyed her. "You do?"

"Of course."

He didn't speak for a moment, then shook his head in disbelief. "You are nothing like what I first thought, Marie."

"What—lifeless and dreary?"

His lips parted in surprise, as if he wasn't sure how to respond. "I-I did apologize for that..."

She smiled. "I know. And I have forgiven you. But that does not mean I won't bring it up any chance I can."

He narrowed his eyes, a distinct spark in them revealing just how delighted he was by her teasing. "Yes, you are very different, indeed."

She smiled, then sobered. "I must share my own apology now, specifically for how mismanaged this entire affair has been. I cannot imagine the shock you must have felt, nor the betrayal. I believe every person ought to have the opportunity to choose whom they wish to wed, and I mourn for you being unable to have that chance. What happened was entirely unjust, and for that, I am sorry."

Charles couldn't speak. For days, he'd longed to hear those words, yearned to know that someone understood him completely. To have Marie of all people speak the exact phrases he needed to hear —to have her comprehend exactly what he'd gone through—he wasn't sure how to feel.

"Thank you," he said, lacing his fingers together. "I've wanted...That is to say, for quite some time, I...Well, thank you."

She eyed him curiously, though nodded in silence.

Neither of them spoke for a moment, Charles still reeling over the burden that Marie had so succinctly removed from around his neck, when another thought occurred.

"May I ask you a question?"

"Yes."

"You have already told me that you were encouraged—not forced—to accept the union between us."

She nodded.

"What was the deciding factor for you to go along with it?"

She looked away. "There were a few reasons, really. The first I'm certain you've already been told." She cast him a sidelong glance. "That I am too old to find a husband of my own now."

He didn't know what to say, unable to deny the truth, but Marie's knowing look silenced him further. "It's true, at any rate. But what really convinced me to go along with the arrangement was the state of my future. I did not relish the prospect of siphoning from my parents' funds for the rest of my days, nor did I wish to spend my future by myself. Such a prospect sounded unbearably lonely."

Charles's heart twisted at her hopeless tone. "And yet," he began softly, hoping to understand her better, "you preferred the idea of growing old with a stranger?"

"I suppose I put a great deal of faith in your mother's description of you." She cast him a knowing glance before continuing. "At any rate, if you recall, we would not have been strangers had you met me before, as was your mother's plan all along. Three times she tried, but you were always busy. Or...you were simply avoiding me."

He squeezed his hands together, attempting not to fidget out of his own discomfort. "Yet something else I must apologize for. I wasn't avoiding you, exactly, as much as I was avoiding *anyone* my mother pushed me towards."

"Yet somehow, she still managed to make the marriage happen."

"She's nothing if not persistent."

They shared another smile before she continued with a small sigh. "After reading your letter, which I assumed was in earnest, I had high hopes that if any man could respond with such enthusiasm to an arranged marriage, I would not mind spending such a future with him."

Charles's heart now doubled over in pain, and he winced. How he regretted that letter. Before, he'd mourned doing so because of how it had affected *him*. Now, he realized how selfish he'd been. His sarcasm toward his mother had affected Marie far more than he'd ever considered.

"Do not begin feeling guilty about that now, too," Marie said, apparently reading his mind.

"It is difficult not to."

"I understand your regret," she stated. "I, too, have experienced a great deal of shame these last few days. Specifically for not pushing my father to renegotiate the wedding when I first discovered your ignorance. I just knew he would never agree to it. He had lost all confidence in my ability to find a husband, and with my reputation ruined, I would have no hope at all."

Charles bit his tongue. The very fact that Mr. Oakley made it known that he'd lost faith in his own daughter was despicable. And yet, Charles, himself, had wondered countless times why she had, indeed, been unable to find a spouse.

He hesitated, not wishing to break the fragile connection now forging between them, but Marie must have seen the question in his eyes anyway.

"You wish to know why I never married," she stated. "The *real* reason why."

Did the woman have some unseen power to read his every thought? "Please forgive my curiosity. You are beautiful, well-accomplished, and can be amenable...when you wish to be."

Her attention snapped to his, and he winked. To his delight, her eyes rounded in surprise, then a blush painted her cheeks. "I could say the same for you, sir."

"Truthfully though, I cannot make sense of it. Your Father shared an explanation of his own at the ball, but I desire to know the truth from your own lips."

His eyes dropped to her mouth at the mention of it.

"If I promise to give you an answer, will you tell me why *you* haven't married?" she asked.

"Of course. I never married because I was too focused on my next big adventure. I knew I would settle down one day, but I wasn't in a hurry. Apparently, my parents thought I was taking too long."

Her lips raised at the corners. "That is precisely what your mother told me, that you were waiting too long to find love."

"Of course she did."

"I hope you will not be angry with her for too long. She means well, though I'm certain you already know that."

Charles did know that, but he couldn't deny he was softened further due to Marie's kindness toward his parents. How could he have ever accused her of misusing them?

"I suppose it is my turn now," she continued. "However, I'm afraid I do not have a straightforward answer for you in regard to why I have remained unmarried for so long. My parents spent many years in London, Bath, and now Surrey in order to find me a husband. I do not boast when I say plenty of gentlemen have expressed interest in me, but the problem was I never had interest in *them*. After the initial attraction, I grew tired of each one, and they, in turn, grew tired of me."

Her eyes took on a far-off look as she stared up into the leaves above them. "My father feared I was too fastidious in attempting to find the perfect gentlemen. But I wasn't looking for perfection. I was looking for friendship. Companionship. *Love*. But love never came. He encouraged me to improve my accomplishments to make up for my age, but in the last year or so, it became clear that once my *advanced years* became known, no gentleman would pursue me beyond safe flirtation in a ballroom." She eyed him with raised brows. "That is why I always enjoyed balls, for there, I could pretend for one blissful evening that my future was not so very bleak after all."

She finished, and Charles was rendered silent. What could he say to make matters better, when he'd only ever proven to make them worse?

She'd wanted the marriage because she could not find love elsewhere—not because no man would love her. And now that she finally had some semblance of security, he'd suggested an annulment. How could he, in good conscience, go through with it now?

But then, she'd said she'd wanted to pursue that course, as well. Unless she'd merely been going along with him to avoid humiliation herself.

He absentmindedly removed his gloves, his palms growing warm as he anticipated her answer. Which reply he preferred, he couldn't be sure. But he knew he needed to find the truth before they spent another day together as husband and wife.

"Marie, do you still wish to remain married?"

Chapter Fifteen

How could Marie answer such a question?

She wished to remain married only if Charles did, but she couldn't bear the guilt that would come if he stayed with her out of obligation rather than his own desire.

"Please be honest," Charles said softly. "We have already made our vows, so you may rest assured I will remain faithful to you until the end."

A lump grew in Marie's throat. This was the sort of man she'd always wanted to marry. Selfless, honorable, kind. If only Heaven had allowed her the opportunity to meet him under different circumstances, ones that didn't include a forced arrangement and an accidental marriage.

But the time for tears had passed. She cleared her throat and pulled on that stoic personality of which Father so approved.

"I am certain we can both agree that neither of us wish to shackle the other in this marriage."

He nodded. "Yes, that is just how I feel."

"Then," she continued, "perhaps we might agree to maintain true to our vows and try a little harder to become friends until Mr. Page writes to you and reveals whatever future awaits us."

Charles appeared to mull over the information. "I suppose

that is the most logical solution. But do you think we are capable of that? Being friends, I mean."

She tipped her head from side to side, as if weighing the options. "Only time will tell. If I were a gambling woman, which I am not, I would say we are far less likely to drive each other mad now."

"Speak for yourself."

He winked at her again, and her stomach dipped with pleasure. If she wished to escape this marriage unscathed, a wink from her husband—who very well could turn out to be *not* her husband—should not affect her in such a way.

In truth, even agreeing to be *friends* with Charles was quite risky.

He straightened on the bench, resting his hands on his thighs. "Well, let us begin anew, then." He stood with his back to her, drew a deep breath that raised his broad shoulders in a movement quite like a barge upon the sea, then turned around to face her once again. His eyes fell on her, and he took a startled step back, holding his gloves in his hands. "Oh, forgive me. I did not see you there. Though, I do not know how I could have missed your beauty."

Marie beamed, though she tried not to. Was this how he would have spoken to her had they met in a more natural manner? She might have scoffed at the ridiculous words, though most likely she would have blushed to high heaven and accepted the compliment with grace.

But they were no longer strangers. And she could behave any way she wished.

She pulled on a frown. "Would you truly speak that way to a woman you just met, Charles?"

He shushed her. "Do not break the illusion," he whispered from the side of his mouth. "Now, may I have your name, Miss..."

Marie grinned. "I am Miss..." She paused, this time with a genuine frown. "Oh, I do not know what name to give you."

"Heavens. Are you unwell? Shall I call for a physician? One should typically know one's own name."

She gave a humored smile. "I am in earnest, Charles. Am I to call myself Miss Oakley, or shall I remain Mrs. Shepherd until...*if* the annulment occurs?"

He pursed his lips in thought. "Very well. You have found another flaw in my little game. Let us simply pick up from where we are right now, yes?"

"That will be far easier," she agreed.

A stronger wind rustled the trees above them, holding a distinct chill that had not been there before.

Charles drew his eyes to the skies east, and Marie followed suit, finding darker clouds mingled with the white.

"I suppose we ought to return before the rain begins," Charles said.

He extended his hand to her, and Marie eyed it for a single moment. She had never accepted his help before—her pride had always prevented her—but seeing as how they were friends now...

She reached forward, sliding her fingers into his hand and instantly regretting her decision to do so.

She had kissed the man already, for heaven's sake. And yet, in some ways, this moment felt more intimate. Perhaps it was due to the fact that she could see his features clearer than she had the night of the ball or because of the way he now watched her—with warmth and a softness of which she didn't know he was capable.

His brown eyes were slightly lighter than she'd first thought, like the color of freshly turned dirt.

He helped her to stand, his thumb resting gently on her knuckles before he tucked her fingers in the crook of his arm. The fabric was warm beneath her hand, though she didn't rest fully upon him. Any further touch would do untold things to her already stuttering heart.

"So. *Marie*," Charles began as they left the church behind and crossed beneath the lych gate. "You have a lovely name. French, is it not?"

The crisp scent of his cologne drifted beneath her nose. "Yes. My great grandmother was French. Mother adored her, so she'd always wished to call her own daughter by the name."

He nodded. "My brother received his name in a like manner. Mother heard the name Tristan when she was on holiday in Wales before he and I were born and fell in love with it. Though it took her longer to concoct my own name."

The Shepherds obviously hadn't intended Marie to marry the second-born twin. Mrs. Shepherd had always said Charles and Marie were far better suited. *"You are just the woman for my Charles—a steady presence, a guiding voice home."*

Was Marie suited for Charles?

"What of your name's meaning?" he asked, interrupting her thoughts.

She rested her hand a little more on his arm.

"Well," she replied, "that depends on who you ask. Some say it means 'star of the sea.'"

"Lovely."

"Yes. Much better than the other."

"Which is...?"

She hesitated. "'Sea of bitterness.'"

He stifled a chuckle. "I can see why you prefer the former."

"Hmm," she mumbled. "I suppose you will be inclined to tease me about that now."

"No," he said, leading her down the lane with an easy stride. "I haven't a leg to stand on when it comes to the meaning of names."

"Why? What does yours mean?"

"You'll find it quite ironic. Charles means, 'free man.'"

Her eyebrows raised in surprise. "That *is* ironic. It would appear that your parents have been duping you all along."

He laughed. "Indeed, they have. Although, Tristan's name means 'sad,' and they couldn't have chosen a word less fitting for my brother."

"Do you two get along well?" she asked.

"Better than well. We spent every day together as children and visit as often as we can now we are adults. It is difficult being away from each other when we are, but I suppose we all have to grow up someday." He gave a small smile. "Well, *I* had to grow up. I may be older, but Tristan was always the more steady and mature of the two of us."

"I should like to see you both together one day," she said. "See how you measure up."

He chuckled, those smile lines around his lips and eyes that she'd seen hinted at over the last couple of days finally apparent.

"I don't know how I feel about you two coming together now," he said. "You might swiftly discover you married the wrong brother."

Marie doubted she could ever think such a thing, for the Charles Mrs. Shepherd had promised had finally arrived, and an annulment from the gentleman was becoming less and less appealing.

The following morning, instead of lingering in her room or *gawking* at Charles from the window—again—Marie made the deliberate decision to leave her room for breakfast.

She knew very likely that Charles would not be there, as he would no doubt be on his usual morning walk. But when she arrived in the dining area, she spotted him already seated at the breakfast table—*and* fully dressed, which she found only marginally disappointing.

Had he chosen to remain indoors due to their conversation yesterday? Warmth stirred in her center.

As her footsteps softly padded into the room, Charles looked up from his plate in surprise, then stood. "I didn't expect to see you this morning. Are you to join me for breakfast?"

"If you'll have me."

"Of course." He waited for her to sit down before taking his seat, as well. His eyes lingered on her as she placed her napkin across her lap. "Did you sleep well?"

"I did," she replied. "And you?"

"As well as I have been able to on that miniscule bed."

She thanked the footman as he placed a cup of tea before her. She felt Charles's eyes on her still as she stirred a cube of sugar into the steaming liquid.

Was he waiting for eye contact? She *could* look up at him...but she rather liked his attention being fixed on her. She didn't want a glance from her to end it prematurely.

Thunder boomed outside, and she nearly started at the unexpected sound. She hadn't even been aware of a storm raging outside, despite the plinking of rain against the glass.

Charles's attention finally shifted from her to the window.

That was why he was indoors. Because of the rain. Not because of her.

She chided her false hope and pulled her declining spirits back up. She shouldn't be wanting such things anyway.

"No walk today, then?" she asked.

"Not in this downpour." He seemed distracted for a moment, then faced her, his shoulders squaring. "But I'm sure we can find something here with which to occupy our attentions."

We. He'd said *we*.

"Unless you'd prefer to remain in your bedchamber again?"

She was surprised to discover that his words weren't dripping with provocation. Instead, vulnerability draped over them—as if he was worried she *would* stay in her room all day.

"I'll stay down here," she said as calmly as possible, though her insides buzzed with joy. "*If* you can behave yourself."

He took a bite of his toast and winked as he chewed. "I'll do my best, Mrs. Shepherd."

Chapter Sixteen

L ater that afternoon, with the rain still pouring from the
skies, Marie retired to the sitting room and was happy to
discover that Charles joined her.

She chose a book from the shelves near the hearth, then sat
down in one of the chairs near the small fire. Her mind refused to
focus on the words, however, her attention arrested by Charles.

From the corner of her eye, she watched his every move. He
stared at her for a moment, peered at the rain against the window,
then stalked to the shelves himself before finding a book and
sitting directly across from her.

From there, he shifted in his seat over and over again, turned
the pages far too swiftly to have read a word, then yawned more
times than she could count.

She stifled a smile. He really was trying, but he very clearly
could not sit still at the moment.

Soon, he gave up entirely, clapping his book shut with a sigh
and slumping forward on the chair with a longing gaze out the
window.

Marie kept her eyes on the pages of her book when Charles
looked at her again, then back out the window, then around the
room.

Poor man. Perhaps there was something she could do to help distract him from his obvious need to expel his energy.

Before she could think of anything, however, Charles twisted around in his seat to face her. "Do I recall you mentioning you play the pianoforte?"

Finally, Marie looked up from the same page she'd been on for the last quarter of an hour. "I do play, yes."

He motioned over his shoulder to where the small pianoforte resided in the far corner of the room. "Care to display one of your many talents for me?"

Marie hesitated. "Oh, I don't know. The instrument does not look as if it has received much playing of late. It would surely need tuning."

He stood, dropping his book on his chair and crossing to the pianoforte. "Could not a talent like you make it sound better?"

"I doubt it."

He glanced over his shoulder. "Now it sounds like you're making excuses. Perhaps you can't even play at all."

She knew he was challenging her, and she had every ability to withstand it. But she was drawn to that twinkle in his eye like a moth to the flame and longed to see it spark even brighter.

Setting her book down in a like manner, she joined him at the pianoforte. She swiped a finger across one of the keys and lifted the layer of dust for Charles to see.

"It will absolutely need tuning," she said.

"Let us see what you can do with it anyway."

He withdrew a handkerchief from his pocket and swiped at the dust, then motioned for her to take her place with a flourish. "Your seat, my lady."

She gave him an exaggerated curtsy, then sat down before the pianoforte. She'd expected Charles to return to his seat, but instead, he remained close to the instrument's side, his hand resting on top of the wood.

Trying to focus on the task at hand instead of Charles's tall, imposing figure, she placed her fingers on the keys and plunked out a little tune, though she winced at every note.

She pulled back, shaking her head at once. "No. This is unplayable."

"Go on. Give it another chance."

She played another few notes. "You won't even be able to recognize the tune."

"Then it shall be a game."

She sighed. "Very well."

She wiggled her fingers, then dove into the song, wincing at each terribly untuned note. At first, she cringed, then the humor of the sound rushed over her, and she laughed.

"This is terrible!" she said.

"I disagree. I've never heard the song before, but it sounds wonderful."

She laughed again. "It is 'The Last Rose of Summer,' Charles. That goes to show how terrible it is if you can't even recognize it."

He chuckled, too, and her giggling picked up, though she continued playing. She couldn't remember the last time she'd laughed like this. She felt light, whole, even healed.

To have Charles's laughter mingled with her own made her feel even better.

Charles knew he was staring, but he couldn't help it. Marie was glowing. He'd never seen her laugh, let alone so heartily. Her smile was luminous, her whole persona so desirable, that the joy overcoming him made him feel...whole.

"I promise I can play better than this," she said through mirthful tears, shaking her head.

Charles believed her. If she could make this pianoforte sound remotely fine, he could hardly wait to see what she could do with a *real* instrument back at Grendale Manor.

The image of Marie in his home, playing his family's

pianoforte, produced a warmth that blossomed in his chest and spread throughout his person.

He had assumed over the last few days that Mr. Page would provide a way for Charles and Marie to end their marriage swiftly. He'd pictured their bridal tour ending prematurely with Marie returning to Westburn and her parents while Charles returned to Grendale.

With Mr. Page's continued silence, that was looking less and less likely—a thought that filled Charles with relief.

But that relief startled him from his thoughts. He *wanted* her to return home with him?

Marie finished the song with another laugh. "Well, there you have it. I told you it would be terrible."

Charles blinked, stretching a smile across his lips. "No, it was wonderful."

She eyed him, having heard the tension in his tone. "Are you all right?"

He nodded, though his movements were too frantic. He was spiraling. He'd been still for too long, and that had allowed his mind to wander and confuse itself.

He wanted to choose his future still. He wanted the annulment still. *Marie* wanted the annulment still. He just needed to remind himself.

"It appears the rain has settled somewhat," he said, though drops still pelted the warped glass. "I think I'll head to the village to see if Mr. Page has written."

Marie's smile faded, but he told himself that could only be a good thing. *They* both needed the reminder.

Still, he did not wish to lose all the progress they had made toward civility. "I would invite you to join me, but I know you only walk in pleasant weather."

She nodded, standing from the instrument and returning to her book. "Yes, that is correct. At any rate, I'd like to continue reading for a time."

Excellent. So they were both content. He lingered a moment

longer, her eyes fixed on the pages of her novel before he finally left the room.

He should have felt instant relief, but all he could think of was how the devil he was going to manage the delicate balance between being there for his wife and not *falling* for his wife.

Please let there be a letter from Mr. Page.

No letter from Mr. Page came that rainy day. Nor the day after that, nor the day after that. On Saturday, a little over a week since arriving at Woewood, Marie sat in the sitting room again on her own, as had become her custom.

Charles walked in—just as *he* always did—with his hat and gloves in his hands and an easy smile on his lips.

"Occupied again?" he asked, motioning to her stitching.

"As always," she said. "Heading to the post office?"

"As always."

They shared a smile, though she kept their eye contact brief as she pulled her attention to the fabric in front of her. The last few days had been comfortable enough. Their conversation had remained civil, if not a little stinted, but she would not murmur. Keeping each other at an arm's length was wise.

He motioned to the window. "The sun is shining this afternoon."

"Mmm. It has been quite some time. It should be very nice for you to not return sodden, I'm sure."

"Indeed." He hesitated. "Would you...would you care to join me?"

Marie poked her finger with her needle but managed to maintain decorum. He was asking her to accompany him? That wouldn't do either of them any good. They spent enough time together as it was. Better to say no. At any rate, he would no doubt enjoy his time walking far better without her.

"That is very kind of you, but I'm afraid I must finish embroidering this handkerchief. I've put it off for far too long."

Charles instantly accepted her pathetic excuse and left with only a silent nod.

Over the next hour, Marie wallowed away in self-pity, frittering from stitching to drawing to letter-writing to reading—before ultimately staring out the window in sullen silence.

She was tormented with thoughts of regret, loneliness, and ruminations about how much better her time would have been had she accompanied him. So despondent she was with her decision to remain at home, as she stared at the roses' shadows on the grass, she determined to never again say no to a request from Charles to join him.

Growing used to his company now would make her life more miserable if their annulment occurred, but at the moment, that was Future Marie's problem. Present Day Marie wanted to relish in the fact that Charles had wished her to come at all.

Finally, when Charles did return, she attempted to remain indifferent.

"Any news from Mr. Page?" she asked.

"I'm afraid not. But you've received a correspondence yourself."

His boots thudded against the wooden floor as he extended the sealed letter to Marie.

She recognized her father's handwriting at once and tore open the seal to read it as Charles made to stand by the window, hands clasped behind his back.

He was no doubt longing to get back out of doors already.

Dearest Marie,

I hesitate writing to you at all when your bridal tour ought to remain the focus of your attention, but I find myself compelled to speak with you on a delicate matter. As such, I trust you will forgive my intrusion.

The night of the ball, I was made aware that you and Mr. Charles Shepherd departed early without a single word of excuse or appreciation to the host and hostess of the party. I need not tell you how ungrateful and improper the slight was, not to mention inconsiderate, as the burden lay upon your mother and myself to make excuses for your poor behavior.

While I'm grateful you and your new husband are bonding, I cannot help but relay instruction in regard to the proper decorum of a married individual. One must learn to control one's appetites—especially in Society—and remember that one's duty is first to one's host before accomplishing the equally important duty of bearing children, which you and Charles are clearly pursuing.

At any rate, I trust you are doing well enough now. We are fine here. Mother is redecorating—

"Marie?"

Marie looked up from the letter, her face aflame as her fingers clenched the paper. Charles watched her, his brow together.

"Are you unwell?" he asked.

"No, I'm...fine."

His eyes dropped to the letter. "Then is someone *else* unwell?"

He must have seen her frowning as she'd read over Father's preposterous assumptions. Honestly, the nerve he had to assume they'd left the ball early to...

"No," she replied, scowling down at the writing once more.

Charles took the seat across from her, pulling it closer so he could meet her eye, but Marie averted her gaze. Father's words were far too humiliating for her to look into Charles's eyes at the moment.

"What is it?" he asked gently.

Marie hid the letter's contents from him.

"You can tell me anything, Marie. We are husband and wife, after all."

Her cheeks pinked further, and she pressed her lips together. She was so ashamed. So...so *humiliated*. She couldn't share the letter with Charles. He'd tease her mercilessly and bring it up whenever he could.

"Ah, yes. Poor, indecorous Marie. Unable to remain at a ball because she could not keep herself from her husband."

And yet, Father's words branded themselves upon her soul, inadvertently lighting a fire of indignation within her that could not be quenched. She may be scorched with the teasing if she released the flames, but at least she wouldn't be burned alive from the inside out.

"It is just that..." She paused, shaking her head. She could not even speak the words. "Here. You may read it. The first few paragraphs."

Charles took the letter, leaning forward to read the words. She shifted uncomfortably in her seat, heat crawling up her body as she imagined Charles's flirtatious grin and mocking laughter.

To her surprise, all he did was frown.

"Your father will soon learn where his opinion is welcome"— he handed the letter back to her—"and where it is unwarranted."

Marie stared at him in shock. "Are you angry?"

He appeared exactly as he had when he'd first met with Father on their wedding day—with scowl lines and rigid lips. "Yes, to be frank, I am. Does he truly believe it is within his right to correct such things—even if they *were* true?" He stood, pacing about the room, his hands fisted at his sides as he continued. "It's ridiculous. You deserve better treatment than that, Marie."

If Marie was shocked before, she was utterly astonished now. He was angry for *her* sake? She'd assumed he was upset due to Father's insinuation of Charles.

"Perhaps I should not have given you the letter," she breathed.

"No, I'm grateful you did. I should not respond with such volatility. But his poor assumption of your good character is..."

He broke off with a gruff sigh. "A father should treat his daughter better than this. He should assume the very best of her."

Marie's mind raced. "It is fine. I am used to such words, really. If he didn't believe me capable of finding my own husband, of course he'd think me incapable of...bridling my actions."

Charles stopped his pacing. "You are used to such words?" he repeated. He shook his head, running his hand against his jawline. "The nerve of the man."

Marie loved Father, though she *had* always thought him to be far too opinionated and a degree too controlling. Still, she did not wish for Charles to lose any sleep over the man. "Really, I'm quite well," she pressed. "I was merely frustrated, that is all." She added with a mumble, "And embarrassed."

Charles eyed her warily, then he sighed, his great shoulders slumping forward. Slowly, he walked toward her, sitting across from her seat and taking both of her hands in his as his dark eyes bore into hers.

"Promise me, Marie," he began. His rumbling voice reverberated from where his fingers grasped hers straight to her heart thumping against her chest. "Promise me that you will not spend one more moment fretting over your father's shameful dishonoring of you. You have nothing to be ashamed of or embarrassed about. My mother and father gave our excuses to the host of the ball, so there was no shame extended toward your parents for our leaving early. This is just your father's way to keep you under his thumb. You do not deserve to be scolded. You deserve to be praised for the noble way you carried yourself through our wedding day—despite everything I put you through. You are a good and honorable woman. Do not let anyone ever convince you otherwise."

Tears sprang to Marie's eyes. She'd been hoping for a bit of understanding, perhaps a pebble of compassion. This staunch defense of who she was as a person was the last thing she'd expected—and the very thing she'd *needed*.

She blinked several times, attempting to swallow the discomfort in her throat at her welling emotion.

He maintained his look, though his voice softened. "And you needn't stop yourself from crying. Tears are the purest form of emotion when produced from the heart."

A tear fled her eyes, and before she could flick it away, Charles reached forward with his thumb and gently brushed her cheek until the moisture was gone.

Their eyes met, and Marie's breath caught in her throat. "Thank you, Charles," she whispered.

He didn't respond for a moment, his gaze lingering on her lips before he cleared his throat and leaned back in his chair. "The nerve of the man," he mumbled under his breath, running his fingers through his hair. "If I ever..."

He stopped, shaking his head and looking at Marie with a deep, settling breath. "Would you do me the honor of accompanying me on a quick walk around the cottage? I find being out of doors helps settle my instability. The sun is still shining, and we do not have to be gone for long. I should like—"

"Yes," Marie said at once. "I would be happy to."

The instant lowering of Charles's shoulders and softening of his brow told Marie everything she needed to know.

She'd made the right decision this time, and she would not regret it.

Chapter Seventeen

After his defense of Marie, Charles felt a palpable shift in their friendship. Where first, he'd been with her out of duty, now he began to look forward to their time together.

Part of this was due to the fact that he was more intentional with his time—refusing to dwell any longer on Mr. Oakley's insolence or fretting about missing the hunting trip with Tristan.

Instead, each morning Charles awakened early, walked for an hour before Marie rose, then returned to Woewood to share breakfast with her—breakfast for which he was always dressed.

From morning on, they spent the rest of each day together, speaking of their families, friends, memories, and interests.

When the weather was poorly, they would remain indoors while Marie read aloud or played the untuned pianoforte for him again, which always proved to send them both into fits of laughter.

Charles had always grown unbearably restless when he was seated indoors all day, but Marie's engaging conversation and enjoyable company caused the hours to fly by unnoticed.

On days when the sun shone, he would request her presence during his walk to the village. Each time, she would readily agree. He assumed her eagerness was due to her desire to find a letter from Mr. Page waiting for them—evidence that she still wished to pursue the termination of their vows. And yet, each time a letter did not arrive, Marie hardly reacted beyond a simple nod, leaving Charles with the impossible task of deciphering if she was upset or pleased.

He knew he ought to ask her again how she felt. But he was too frightened to do so—just as he was too frightened to untangle his own web of befuddled feelings on the subject.

With Mr. Page's continued silence, Charles's sense of urgency and desperation for the annulment had lessened to a degree, replaced with a grating discomfort at both the thought of staying within the marriage *and* ending it.

Charles loved his old life. Spending time with his friends had been his greatest joy for many years. And yet, deep down, he'd always known something was amiss.

He'd first perceived this void within him when he'd spent time with Andrew and his new bride—and with Thomas and his wife. They seemed so happy, so content. Charles had never experienced any such feelings, always having to chase one experience after another to distract himself from his empty boredom—and his empty life.

So now, to be perfectly content merely *sitting* with Marie, to revel in the rewarding sound of her lilting laughter and witnessing her smiles, looks, and goodness firsthand...he had to question what exactly he *was* feeling. Belonging? Satisfaction? Wholeness?

He still longed for freedom and for a happy future with a wife of his choosing, but he could not deny how greatly he enjoyed *Marie's* bright company. The thought of no longer having her in his life lowered his spirits to an almost crushing level.

He prevented himself from dwelling too long on these perplexing and often shifting emotions, but each night after he and Marie finally parted well after ten in the evening, his thoughts always centered on her.

Even that night, five days later, he thought of her as he lay in bed half-dressed, staring up at the shadows the fire cast upon his ceiling. With his feet crossed at the ankles, he shifted his legs back and forth, waiting impatiently for what was to come.

Finally, eleven o'clock appeared on his pocket watch, and Charles heard the first, soft sounds of Marie's gentle singing from her bedchamber, just as it had each night since their conversation at the church.

He eyed the old, wooden wall separating them, imagining her lips as she sang the lyrics to whatever song she chose that evening. From what he could tell, she stood near her window as she sang, peering through the glass while brushing out her long, black locks.

Of course, this was all conjecture, for Charles had never seen her do such a thing. But oh, how he could imagine it.

He closed his eyes as her soft tone continued, her smooth, unassuming voice encompassing him. The muted brushing continued, and he could almost see her silken tresses draping like a dark waterfall over the shoulder of her dressing gown. How long did her hair flow? Past her waist? Did it feel as smooth as it always appeared?

Thinking of a woman in this manner was hardly gentlemanly, and yet, did not a husband have permission to think of his wife in such a way?

Perhaps if she was to *remain* his wife...

He frowned. The thought had come in tandem with listening to Marie singing each night. It was moments like these, in the late hour where his will weakened and his mind wavered enough for him to dare to think the impossible—that living with Marie as his wife might not be as terrible as he'd first thought.

He attempted to push the notion aside, but her voice continued to wrap around his heart. How he longed to actually *see* her singing.

"Father said I am far more accomplished in playing pianoforte," she'd said to him after Charles requested her to sing along as she played.

His heart ached at the thought of Mr. Oakley not approving

of her. She deserved a father's approval. Just as she deserved a husband's approval.

Just as she deserved to fall in love. Dare Charles think she could ever fall in love with him?

He opened his eyes, staring at the dark ceiling as the intrusive thoughts continued, for he was no longer able to ward them off.

Marie was everything Mother had always promised. Accomplished, charming, thoughtful, beautiful, sensitive. Indeed, with only a few days left of their bridal tour, he found himself unready to share her once more with reality.

And yet, Charles still hesitated committing his future to her. He had longed to marry someone with whom he could enjoy the outdoors. Someone to take riding, to roll down fields together, to boat into the middle of a lake with. As much as he enjoyed his time with Marie indoors or their simple walks to the village, he feared that one day he would grow restless. Then what? Would he remain indoors to keep Marie company forevermore? Or was there any chance at all for her to find joy in the activities in which *he* partook?

For years, he'd had an image in his mind that involved his future family sharing in adventures together. But no matter how he tried, he could not imagine Marie fitting into the ideal portrait he had painted.

As calming an effect as her presence had had on him, he knew deep down he could not change something so fundamental about himself as his desire to be out of doors—just as he knew Marie would not change who *she* was inside.

If their marriage remained intact, he would have to give up his adventuring altogether or do so alone, all while accepting the remorse that would inevitably follow should he ever leave Marie on her own, for he knew her loneliness would be his doing.

The singing stopped, and Charles waited, running his fingers through his hair with bated breath. When Marie began again, this time with a slower, more somber song, his brow drew together at the ache that arose in his chest.

He was never supposed to have fallen for her. And now, after complaining and criticizing and reneging on his promises for so long, he hardly knew what to do with himself.

Yes, you do, Charles.

He pushed the niggling thought away, but the harder he pressed, the more it pestered him again and again until finally, his fatigue overcame him.

He knew what he needed to do. But he simply did not have the fortitude to do it.

With defeated spirits, he allowed his arms to fall down at his sides. His feet ended their tapping, his mind stopped its racing, and his heart ceased its longing for something he could not have.

He was empty, void of effort and desire—for no matter which path forward he took, he would be left wanting.

All that was left to comfort him now was his darkened room and the hope that Marie's singing would last until he fell fast asleep, for at least then he might receive respite.

Chapter Eighteen

The following morning, a fortnight after they had arrived at Woewood, Marie and Charles made their way to the village for their daily walk.

Marie peered up at him as she held his arm, the two of them walking down the lane in silence.

"Is everything all right?" she asked after a moment.

Charles didn't seem himself that morning. Shadows clung to his under-eyes, and his stride felt more rigid.

He blinked, seeming to come out of a deep reverie. "Of course. Why do you ask?"

She raised a shoulder. "You seem...quiet."

"My apologies. I suppose I am simply preoccupied with my thoughts."

He offered nothing further, so she *asked* nothing further. A soft rumbling of thunder drew her attention behind them, and she glanced back to see dark clouds on the horizon.

"Oh, perhaps we ought to return to Woewood before that storm arrives," she said.

Charles peered over his shoulder. "We can if you wish to, but I'm certain we will have plenty of time to make it to the village and back before it sets in."

She nodded, following his lead forward. They walked together in silence, and Marie chewed on her lower lip as another thunder rumbled. She glanced back, though Charles remained clearly unbothered.

"You're certain we will not be caught in it?" she asked.

He eyed her, his brow puckered with confusion. "Caught in —Oh, the storm? Well, I cannot be certain of it, but I am *nearly* certain of it. At any rate, we are both dressed warmly enough, and a few drops of rain never hurt anyone."

He smiled reassuringly, then faced forward again.

Marie tried to be as unconcerned as he was, but the thought of being doused with rain hardly sounded appealing. All those wet underclothes and such. Falling into the fountain had been a terrible experience—though it had been made worth it by what happened beforehand. Perhaps getting caught in a storm with Charles wouldn't be so very bad if they...

She pushed the thought from her mind, refocusing her energy on Charles, who'd fallen silent again. "Care to share of what you are thinking so deeply?"

He helped her step around a large puddle in the middle of the lane. "I was thinking of my friends."

Her stomach tossed with unease. "What about them?"

"Merely the hunting trip I was supposed to take with Tristan and the visit I was supposed to make to Leonard Stanton after that."

Marie had been afraid of this. She typically avoided speaking of his friends, for it brought up all that Charles had given up for her. But then, perhaps speaking of them now would allow her to clarify a few matters.

"Charles," she began, "if we cannot pursue the annulment, and our marriage must remain intact, I wish you to know that you do not have to give up the life you led before. You can still do all that you wish to do, and I will be perfectly content to remain at home. I'll have your mother and father for companions, so I shall not be so very lonely should you desire to take your leave."

To her surprise, one side of his mouth raised in a smile. "I do not know if you are aware of what you're offering me, Mrs. Shepherd."

She tipped her head to the side. "What do you mean?"

"Do you know what sort of life I led before?"

"You were away from home often, though I do not know why."

"I was house-hopping"—he cast her a sidelong glance—"to avoid my mother's matchmaking."

Marie smiled. "You weren't very good at it."

"No, indeed. But no man is a match for her will."

"Did you have a favorite place to stop in?"

He thought for a moment. "I quite liked staying with my friend Rowan at Ashworth Hall. They have a lovely river nearby and an extensive library."

"You *enjoy* reading?" She smiled at the memory of his inability to read a single page of the book he'd chosen only days before.

"I do enjoy it, but only when outside."

"I should have known. Do any of your friends ever come to stay with you at Grendale?"

"They daren't. Mother would have them all married off by the end of the visit."

Marie laughed. "Well, you needn't worry about that for yourself any longer. Unless Mr. Page brings news today, that is."

"I suppose you're right. But you may rest assured, if we do remain married, I shan't be partaking in the activities I was beforehand."

"Which were..." she prompted. "Other than house-hopping, I mean."

"Nothing untoward, I assure you. Merely your average gentlemanly pursuits. Monthlong hunting trips, fishing for weeks at a time, grand tours around Europe."

Marie stared. "You went on The Grand Tour?"

"Indeed."

"How did you manage that with the wars?"

"We traveled toward the end of 1810. We were kept safe for the most part, though on our return journey, it was not enemy ships that nearly brought us to our deaths but a terrible storm. We were all quite worried—even I was, though I hid it better than the others." He smiled as he clearly relived the experience. "They were convinced their deaths were at hand, hence why they made the wager."

"Wager?"

Charles's lips parted in surprise. "Oh, yes. We...we made a wager that the last of us to marry would owe the other men a hundred pounds each."

Her brow raised. "Heavens. That's quite the expensive wager."

"Indeed."

"And you *weren't* in a rush to marry?"

He chuckled. "No, I knew I would do so eventually. At any rate, *no one* was in a hurry. Most of us set the wager aside as merely good fun until Thomas married. He sent us a letter, reminding us of the deal, so the pressure has been felt by all now."

Marie smiled at the silliness of it all. Only men would ever think to do such a thing. "Is he the only one to have married thus far?"

"No, Andrew Langford married his lifelong love only recently. Though how that marriage came about is another delightful story entirely, as he practically fell into it. His wife matches him in intelligence and wit, though, which he desperately needed. I believe they are quite happily matched. Other than those two, the rest of us remain unattached. The rest of *them*, I should say."

His smile slowly faded, and guilt racked Marie's conscience.

"I'm sorry," she said softly. "I'm sorry you've had to give up so much for this marriage."

He stopped walking to face her. "I do not blame you, you know. I did in the beginning, but I was wrong to do so, for none of this is your doing."

"I suppose you're right. Our parents were both determined to see it through."

He looked away. "Just as we are determined to end it."

Her heart sank, though she nodded in agreement all the same.

When they reached the village, Marie spent a moment at the haberdashers, looking through the ribbons while Charles went to the post office on his own.

Despite her best efforts, she simply could not focus on trivial matters such as ribbons and bonnets and trimmings, so she left the shop behind to wait for Charles's return in the cool, spring air.

As she did so, she caught sight of the doorpost at the inn, an advertisement posted in thick letters standing out above the rest.

Maidstone Market Day
Third Week in March
Vendors, Entertainers, Animals, Food

Her mind churned over the information, though it fled as she turned and spotted Charles walking in her direction through the small crowds. His eyes moved from person to person until he finally met her gaze, and his features brightened.

Marie's breath caught. He looked pleased to see her, a skip in his step and a smile on his lips that was finally genuine.

That could mean only one thing. He'd finally received a letter.

With an unpleasantly racing heart, she waited for him to reach her, pulling up her courage.

"You received a letter from Mr. Page," she stated before he could say a word.

His features fell. "Oh, yes. I have."

Was he attempting to hide his joy at the mere thought of leaving her?

"And," she pressed, "what did he say?"

He pulled the folded paper from his jacket pocket, then extended it to her.

Mr. Charles Shepherd,

*I regret to inform you that my source has yet to write back
with any word as to your inquiry. I suspect he has simply
not understood the haste I requested.*

*At any rate, I have been tasked to meet with Tristan while I
am in London, so I will make discreet inquiries whilst
there.*

Until then, enjoy your latest adventure,

Mr. Barnabas Page

Was that it? Marie had more than expected a resolution, what
with Charles's reaction upon seeing her. Unless he was pleased
that there was no news yet.

"Well," she said, breathless at the thought, "there's that,
then."

Charles averted his gaze. "I'm sorry to say we will have to wait
a few days more for our futures to be settled."

"I suppose we shall."

He offered his arm to her, and together they left the village.
Instead of maintaining his disconcerting silence, Charles seemed a
degree happier, whether that was due to renewed hope or something else, she couldn't decipher.

"So," he said, as if they were in the middle of a conversation,
"we've spoken a number of times about my own adventures. Now
we must speak of yours."

Marie balked. "*My* adventures? I hardly believe I need to tell
you I do not partake in any."

"Nonsense. Mr. Page's letter said, well, never mind that now. I
believe that any experience—great or small—can be seen as an
adventure, depending on how one views it. Not all journeys may

look alike. My escapades may appear different than yours, but that does not mean yours are any less exciting."

Marie tried to keep up with his swift words. "I suppose."

"So what in your life has been exciting?"

Pressure mounted on Marie's shoulders. "I assure you, I have done nothing compared to you."

"No, do not compare it with me. What have *you* done that *you* have found exciting?"

Marie racked her brain for something to impress Charles, but with every idea, she fell short. Playacting before her parents, racing across the countryside on foot when she was a child, climbing to the top of a tree when she was a young woman—all of them seemed so very lackluster compared to his house-hopping and grand-touring.

Charles remained silent as she continued thinking, though a smile lingered on his lips as he watched her expectantly.

"Well," she began, finally settling on one, though she still wasn't impressed with the memory herself, "I once ran away from home—just for the day, mind—so that I might attend a festival at harvest time. Mother and Father found it too base, but I wished to attend, so I snuck out in the morning and danced and played and ate all day." She ended with a shrug. "That was exciting to me."

She braved a glance at Charles and was relieved to find complete joy written across his features.

"I did the very same when I was a boy," he said, his eyes bright. "Tristan pretended to be me so I could escape flute lessons at home. To this day it remains one of my fondest memories, that festival."

Marie gleamed.

The advertisement she'd seen in the village crossed her mind again, and her smile grew as an idea was planted in her thoughts.

In the next moment, however, thunder rumbled directly above, and Marie looked up, stunned to see the storm clouds she'd been fretting about before, now directly upon them.

"*Nearly* certain we wouldn't be caught in it?" she asked. "Isn't that what you said?"

He grinned sheepishly. "Well, think of it this way. You shall now have another adventure to add to your list."

She looked at him with suspicion as the first drop fell. "Was this your plan all along?"

"As if *I* plan that far ahead," he said with a laugh. Another drop fell, then another. "Worry not, we will be home before it falls too hard."

And yet, in the next moment, the clouds opened, and water poured forth from seemingly every inch of the skies above.

"Or not," he said, wincing as the rain pelted against them.

"Now what?" she asked, her voice raised to be heard above the sheets of rain.

She lifted a hand, though it did even less than her bonnet in shielding her face from the droplets.

"Now we make a run for it," he said.

The look of excitement across his features caused her to laugh despite herself. He clasped her hand with his and barreled down the lane, his pace steady for her to keep up as she raised her skirts and ran alongside him.

"Are you well?" he called out over his shoulder.

Getting caught in the rain with Mother had always been a chore—listening to her complaints and fears of catching a cold. But getting caught in the rain with Charles?

Marie smiled. "Never better!"

The look he gave her was worth all the discomfort in the world.

Within just a few minutes, they arrived at the cottage, clambering beneath the small awning and the shelter it provided.

They stood side-by-side, catching their breath and staring out at the rain. Charles removed his gloves, then hat, running his fingers through his mostly dry hair with another chuckle.

"That *was* an adventure." He peered down the length of her. "You are even wetter than you were from the fountain."

She laughed, feeling not one ounce of shame over her appearance, for Charles's look of approval was apparent.

"I'm certain this isn't helping my case for getting you to enjoy being out of doors," he said.

But Marie shrugged. "I'm beginning to learn that one's enjoyment of matters is entirely dependent upon one's company."

A smile passed between them, though she ended it prematurely to remove her bonnet. "Although, you do know I shall now never trust your weather predictions. Nor you personally, should we ever again be within close proximity to a fountain."

"There you go again," he said, watching her every movement, "blaming me for our little dip in the fountain when it was more your fault than anyone's." He gave a shake of his head. "It is a wonder you trusted me enough to get you back to Grendale safely. I thought for certain you would have left me for your parents that night."

"I made a vow, Charles. A simple fountain mishap and argument was not going to change that."

He sobered, and only then did she realize what her words had insinuated.

"Until...until we know what comes of the annulment," she managed.

"Of course."

His eyes searched hers, his brow soft. "I think of that night often."

Rain clicked upon the stone pathway leading to the house, and droplets bounced from the pink and red rose petals beside them. The world was cloaked in a gentle, muted grey, but the space around Marie and Charles glowed brightly.

"You mean the night of the ball?" she asked, her eyes fixed on him.

"The ball...and the gardens afterward."

She swallowed. "An argument like that is hard to forget."

A spare drop of rain ran down his temple. "I wasn't thinking of the argument."

"What, then?"

"Can you truly not know?"

Of course she knew, for she had thought of their kiss a hundred times over.

That kiss had been filled with anger and frustration. With disappointed hopes and dreams. And yet, her desire for Charles had yet to be silenced, and the stirring in her heart to be close to him had never been satiated.

Even now, as his eyes centered on her lips, heat burst within her, for she could feel his own longing as well—that pull, that craving to experience just one more moment of affection.

But this time, if they did kiss, it would not be filled with anger. This time, the kiss would be shared between two people who had drawn closer to each other...but who had promised to keep away.

He drew a step closer, and her eyes threatened to flutter closed, but she had to keep her wits about her. "Charles..."

"Tell me you have not thought of that moment yourself," he whispered, ignoring her weak attempt at protest.

Marie fought off her response for as long as she could, but it was to no avail. "I have. I do."

"And do you regret the moment we shared?"

She raised her chin, an invisible force pulling her toward him. "I do not. Do you?"

"How could I? It is all I have thought of since. I have never experienced a kiss like that one."

"Due to my anger?"

He quirked a smile. "Due to what awakened within me."

"And what was that?"

She should not be encouraging him. They had made the promise to keep away from each other. But then, what if he no longer wished to pursue the annulment? What if...what if he was falling in love with her?

Her head began to spin as he leaned toward her.

"What awakened within me was the desire to see what a true

kiss might feel like between us. One where both of us give it freely."

Oh, how she wanted to experience the very same.

But *one* of them had to be the voice of reason. "What of the annulment? If we continue on this path, we may end up with a life neither of us has chosen."

He stared down at her. "What if it is a life we *both* choose?"

What was he saying—that he wanted to give their marriage a chance? She already knew that was what *she* wanted. They'd experienced more in their mere week of knowing one another than most couples did in a lifetime—quarrels and kisses. Tears and apologies. Friendship and forgiveness. Dare she hope he might want to pursue a relationship with her where joy and love might be discovered in the end?

With a deep breath, she nodded. "What if it is," she stated without question.

That was all Charles needed, for in the next moment, he leaned toward her, and Marie closed her eyes, waiting for his kiss to once again be hers.

Chapter Nineteen

Charles's breathing grew labored at the feel of Marie's breath on his lips—one final whisper of air before this remarkable woman and her affection would be his.

But when the door latch clicked beside them, the heavy wood swinging open with a creak, he and Marie took a deliberate step away from each other to face the culprit who had ended their kiss before it had even begun.

Charles stared at the interloper, ready to rage, but instead, he fell into stunned silence. There, within the doorway of the cottage, stood his brother.

"Well, well, well," Tristan said with a broad smile, "what do we have here?"

"Tristan?" Charles finally forced out. "What the devil..."

Tristan laughed, reaching forward to clasp Charles's shoulders in an embrace. Charles returned it, though he pulled back with more confusion than ever.

"What are you doing here?" he asked as the three of them shuffled into the small entryway, leaving the rain—and his abandoned kiss with Marie—behind.

"Surprised?" Tristan asked. "Not as greatly as I am, I can assure you."

His eyes fell on Marie with a studious gaze, though his smile remained bright.

Charles fell silent as the situation settled upon him. Mother and Father had requested that the details of the arrangement remain secret so they might not frighten Tristan from coming home.

But how could Charles lie to his own brother? And yet, if he did share with Tristan how upsetting this whole arrangement had been, would that not injure Marie? Not necessarily her reputation, but her heart?

He could not put her through that again.

With squared shoulders, he made his decision.

"I take it you received my letter," Charles said with a glance in Marie's direction.

She stood still and silent, though a small smile graced her lips —those lips he'd almost tasted of once more.

Focus, Charles.

"Indeed, I did," Tristan replied. "After receiving your cancellation of our hunting trip, I knew you had to be in earnest. Nothing would make you cancel such an outing. I returned to Grendale straightaway and spoke with Mother and Father first. They didn't hesitate to tell me how madly in love the both of you had fallen after a mere day of being with one another, so I simply had to see it for myself."

Charles drew a deep breath. This was it. He placed a hand at the small of Marie's back. "It is true. We are married. Tristan, I believe you know my lovely wife, Marie. Marie, my brother, Tristan."

A few pleasantries were exchanged, then nothing else followed. Charles looked between them, his tongue frozen in place.

Marie was right. He was terrible at playacting.

Instinctively, he glanced at her for help.

It was as if a candle had been lit within a dark room, her expression shifting instantly. She straightened her back and pulled a bright smile upon her features as she directed her attention to Tristan.

"I am so happy to see you again, sir," she said graciously. "Though I feel I know more about you now than I did before, thanks to Charles. I do hope the fact that I am at fault for his cancellation of your hunting party will not sully your opinion of me before we have had the opportunity to get to know one another better. I assure you, should any event arise in the future, I shall highly encourage your brother to attend."

Tristan appeared pleasantly surprised by her words, though Charles was even more so. He'd seen Marie shift from stoic to honorable, from conversational to silent, and from flirtatious to angry. This was a side to the woman he hadn't seen until now—the comfortable and secure hostess.

He couldn't deny how appealing it was.

"I assure you," Tristan responded, "nothing will sully my opinion of the woman who has managed to win favor with Charles."

"What a relief," she said. Then she turned to Charles.

Once more, his mind emptied of all potential words.

"Oh, ignore him," Tristan said, "As you can see, I've startled my brother into a stunned silence." He shrugged. "I'm sure he'll come around soon."

Marie laughed. "It takes a great deal to silence him. I commend you for your quick work."

Tristan chuckled, clearly impressed with her repartee. "I'll give you a few suggestions if you're interested. Might come in use throughout your life."

"Oh, please, do."

Charles watched the exchange in silence, half-annoyed with their teasing, half-pleased with how well they were getting on.

He wasn't certain why it was so important to him that they did, but he knew a sense of relief to see it all the same.

Silence fell, and Charles realized that both of them were watching him again expectantly.

Instead of relying on him to speak—or rather, not to speak—Marie placed a gentle hand on his upper arm. "What a sight we must be, my dear. Appearing so sodden will hardly add to my favor." She gave a little laugh. "You must excuse me, Tristan, for my appearance. Your brother has allowed us to become caught in the rain—drew it up as some sort of adventure." She shared a knowing smile with Tristan. "At any rate, I shall freshen up, then perhaps the three of us can take tea in the sitting room just through there."

"That would be lovely," Tristan said.

Charles again remained silent, caught up in Marie's very presence. Was this what life with her would look like if they were truly in love and remained married? Would she play hostess to his friends and family, be kind and loving—offer to care for them and become friendly with them of her own accord?

He couldn't deny the appeal of such a life. There was something compelling about the image, something feminine about Marie instantly caring for her guest and his brother, that the desire to be cared for himself awakened within Charles's soul.

"Charles?" she asked.

He blinked out of his reverie, clearing his throat. "Yes, I should like to change into dry clothes, as well. Do excuse us, Tristan."

"Of course."

Tristan eyed them with a scrutinizing gaze before leaving for the sitting room on his own.

Marie stared after him with a small smile. "I like him," she said softly, then she promptly turned toward the stairs.

What had she meant by that? Did she *like* him, or was she merely amused by him? That unwelcome feeling of jealousy he'd grown so accustomed to knocked once more at his door, but Charles didn't answer. Tristan was a flirt, but he knew boundaries—and Marie was Charles's wife.

"Are you well?" Marie asked from over her shoulder as he followed behind her up the steps.

He had to avert his gaze from what was directly in front of him. "I'm...well enough."

In truth, he wasn't well at all. He couldn't speak—not only due to his inability to lie, but also due to the shifting emotions and feelings within him. He felt as unstable as a ship rocking about at sea.

They reached the top step, and she cast him a smile over her shoulder as she opened the door to her bedchamber. "Do not tarry. Heaven knows what he'll think we're up to if we take too long."

Her eyes lingered a moment on his lips, then she entered her room and closed the door promptly behind her.

Charles stood there for a moment, blowing out a slow breath and holding his hands at the back of his head. He stared at the door handle. Had she not locked it on purpose?

He took a step toward it, then shook his head and made for his room instead.

No tarrying, indeed.

Within a matter of moments, both he and Marie were sitting with Tristan, enjoying tea and Shrewsbury biscuits as they warmed themselves by the small fire.

Charles remained on edge as he listened to Tristan share all of the goings-on in London—where Tristan typically housed in their family townhome to avoid Mother's meddling—for he knew what conversation was being kicked down the road.

Sure enough—and far too soon—they arrived at what he'd been dreading.

"Well, that is enough about me," Tristan said, leaning back in his chair as he finished off the last of his biscuit. "I wish to hear more about the both of you. Last I heard, Charles, you hadn't ever had the privilege of meeting Marie before this week, unless I'm mistaken."

Charles was about to avert his gaze, but Tristan caught him before he could. All at once, he knew Tristan was aware of the truth. They'd never been able to keep secrets from one another, but Charles had hoped, for Marie's sake, that just this once, he'd be able to keep his mind to himself.

So much for that.

Still, Charles had to maintain the façade for the comfort of his wife.

"It all happened rather suddenly," he said stiffly.

"May I ask how?" Tristan asked in a clear challenge.

"Have you not told him yet?" Marie asked before Charles could falter again. She gave an amused shake of her head. "Never trust a man to share the details. He is right, though. Everything did happen rather suddenly. Well, from his perspective, at least. The poor man put off meeting me for over a year. When we did finally manage to meet, there was no denying a marriage was in our future."

She was remarkable, really. The way she spun her words to never tell a falsehood.

"Sounds like a dream," Tristan said, clearly not buying Marie's explanation. He faced Charles again. "I cannot believe I wasn't informed in more detail of all that had occurred."

Charles opened his mouth, but again, nothing came.

"That surprises you?" Marie asked with a laugh. "Is Charles not the worst communicator? Never responding to his parents' letters, never returning home. I am unsurprised in the least that nothing else was mentioned before now."

Poor Marie was doing her best, but she had no hope with Tristan's astuteness.

Still, his brother remained kind. "That is true. I was surprised he even informed me of his canceling the hunting party."

They shared a laugh, and even Charles smiled before Tristan's condemning eyes reached his again.

"It is all rather strange, though," he said with a shadowy tone. "Is it not?"

Charles's chest tightened. Tristan was not pleased with all this trickery. Nor was Charles. But he could not injure Marie.

Please, he pleaded with his eyes. *Let it be, brother. I will explain soon.*

Only a second passed before Tristan gave a subtle nod, having obviously caught on to Charles's request.

He drew a deep breath, and his analyzing eyes softened. "Strange, though not unbelievable," he said with a smile.

"I was sorry that you could not be in attendance for the ceremony, though," Marie said, sobering. "I fear my parents were the ones responsible for the swiftness of our vows, though that does not mean I do not regret the lack of those in attendance."

Tristan nodded. "Thank you, sister," he said with a twinkle in his eye at the final word. "But I understand, of course. We must do what it takes to maintain the happiness of our parents."

Tristan sent Charles a knowing look, and finally, the tension between his shoulders eased.

The conversation finally shifted as Tristan eased off, and soon, Marie leaned forward in her seat.

"I believe dinner will be ready soon. I do hope you will join us, brother."

"I would be happy to."

"Excellent. I should like to hear your take on this story of the storm on the sea during your Grand Tour. Apparently, Charles said he was the bravest of you all, but I should like a second opinion on the matter."

Tristan chuckled, and Marie stood, the men following suit. "Now, if you'll excuse me. I shall make ready for dinner and ensure another place is set. Though you must excuse our small table. There may be some bumping of the knees if we are not careful."

She smiled, then left the room.

Charles and Tristan sat down, and finally, the stress from the conversation melted away as he faced his brother with a heavy sigh.

Tristan folded his arms and faced him directly, and Charles fought his urge to squirm. "Thank you," he whispered.

"For what, not condemning you and your wife for the amount of lies you've just told your own brother?" His words were harsh, but his tone was light.

"Forgive me," Charles said with a wince. "I am stuck between two corners—my brother's and my wife's. I will defend her honor, though, by saying she did not speak a single untruth with her words. However, I should like to tell you the full truth now, should you wish to hear it."

"Oh, it is the greatest desire of my life as of this moment," Tristan said. "I don't know what would lead you to marriage other than the fact that you've truly fallen in love, that Mother blackmailed you into this, or that some scandal occurred and you couldn't keep your hands off the woman."

Heat crawled up Charles's neck. Truthfully, the latter would have been more plausible had he met Marie on his own.

Standing up, he closed the door, then returned to Tristan with the full tale of all that had occurred, including their decision to annul the marriage—though he did leave out their little swim in the fountain and the preceding kiss.

When he finished, relief pulled a yawn from his lips. "So there you have it. What say you?"

To his surprise, Tristan merely smiled.

"What, you find it all humorous?" Charles asked on the defensive.

Tristan's lack of empathy was beginning to sound dangerously close to their parents'.

"Not how it all came about," Tristan clarified, soothing Charles's concerns. "That is terrible, though not entirely implausible. But that is not why I smile."

"Then why do you?" Charles asked.

Once again, Tristan's grin took residence on his lips. "I hate to tell you this, Charles, but Mother was right. I have never met a woman more perfect for you than Marie."

Chapter Twenty

A fluttering occurred in Charles's chest at the words, though he wasn't ready to give in quite yet. "Don't be ridiculous."

"I'm not, and you know it," Tristan said. "She is the perfect calm to your chaos. Your equal in looks and accomplishments. Your comrade in arms. And look at the way she instantly came to your rescue after your pathetic attempt to lie. She is your better half, whether you admit it or not."

Charles refused to listen. "Those are weighty statements, seeing as how you hardly know the woman."

"You hardly know her either," Tristan said. "And yet, you've already fallen for her."

Charles made a sound of disbelief, but it sounded weak even to his own ears. "Well, it doesn't matter anyway. We're still seeking an annulment."

Tristan's smile faded. "You can't be serious."

"I am. Mr. Page will be getting back to us shortly. He's speaking with a friend of his who specializes in annulments as a solicitor in London. I expect he'll send word any day now that will help us find a way out of this predicament that will leave us both unscathed."

Now who was being ridiculous? Charles could have laughed

at his preposterous words. He knew now more than ever that an annulment would not ever be granted in tandem with the promise of Marie's reputation remaining intact.

But more than that, he was ridiculous in choosing to believe that he still wanted to end the marriage.

Seeing Marie with Tristan, seeing her as the lady of the house who came to his aid, had solidified that knowledge. As had Mr. Page's writing from before.

"Enjoy your latest adventure."

Those words had shaken loose Charles's bonds. He'd been looking at life through foggy spectacles, blinding him to reality. His marriage to Marie *was* an adventure—and she was standing right beside him, willing to take part in that adventure, too.

She was someone who could be relied upon. Someone who could be a helpmeet to him. Someone he could fall desperately in love with. What more could a man ask for in a wife?

"You're a fool, Charles."

Charles averted his gaze. "I know it."

"Then why do you still cling to the annulment?" Tristan asked, his voice low. "What is stopping you from jumping forward with her?"

Charles cursed their twin connection. Once again, Tristan could see into his very thoughts. There *was* something holding him back.

"She said she never would have chosen to marry me," he finally voiced aloud. "She fully agreed to the annulment. The last thing I'd wish for is to be married to a woman who feels obligated to remain with me. She deserves more than that. She deserves—"

He stopped abruptly at Tristan's growing smile.

"What?" Charles asked.

"Oh, nothing. It is just nice to hear you talk this way about a woman, that is all. When your letter first arrived, I thought you'd gotten married to avoid paying the rest of us."

Charles gave a mirthless laugh. "I'm certain that's what they'll all think."

"Until they see you with veritable stars in your eyes each time you speak of your wife."

Charles looked away, knowing he had them in his eyes now. "If I do remain married, that only means the pressure mounts for the rest of you. Unless you already have a woman you're pursuing?"

"I have many women. You know me."

But there was something in his tone that gave Charles reason to pause. *Was* Tristan pursuing some*one*?

"Perhaps if you're daft enough to pursue the annulment, I'll go after Marie myself."

His brother's words knocked Charles's curiosity from his brain. Tristan was teasing, but the very thought of such a union caused his stomach to revolt.

"Oh, he doesn't like that," Tristan goaded.

Charles scoffed, then looked away to hide his growing annoyance. He was ready to be finished with this part of the conversation now.

"All would be easier if Mr. Page would simply respond with a firm answer," he said. "Then I could know if we are to end this or not."

"Or," Tristan began, "all would be easier if you made the decision to do everything within your power to encourage Marie to fall in love with you."

Charles's eyes swung up to meet Tristan's.

Encourage Marie to fall in love with him. That *was* an idea. They were to return in just two days' time to Grendale, and being back with his parents and the rest of Society would certainly make it more difficult to draw closer. He knew she was attracted to him, but was it possible—had he any hope at all—that she might fall for him as he was falling for her?

He supposed there was only one way to find out.

Tristan left for London shortly after dinner, and Marie and Charles stood in the doorway together, waving goodbye until he disappeared into the darkness.

"He knew, didn't he?" Marie asked, not wasting a single moment.

Charles hesitated. "He did."

Just as she suspected.

Dinner had been pleasant and peaceful. The very fact that Tristan had watched her with curiosity instead of suspicion proved that he was fully aware of their relationship being an act. She suspected he knew all along, but she *knew* Charles had told him the truth when she'd left them in the sitting room, which was the very reason she *had* left—to allow them an opportunity to speak.

Still, it was fun to playact all night as if she and Charles were happily wedded. How unfortunate to end it now.

"It was nothing you did that made him aware," Charles said, turning to face her.

"Oh, I know that. It was your stiff delivery of every single line."

He chuckled. "Just so."

The candlelight from inside flickered across his features, and she traced the angle of his jaw with her eyes. "Charles?"

"Yes?"

"I have something to ask you." She hated how vulnerable she sounded, but the brightness within his expression encouraged her to continue. "Something...I wish to do."

His eyes searched hers, his head tipped with intrigue.

"Would you like to come with me somewhere tomorrow?"

A soft smile curved his lips upward. "I'd be happy to. But might I inquire as to where?"

She shook her head, her courage growing. "No, it is a surprise."

"A surprise? Then I absolutely will join you."

"Good. We must leave tomorrow morning. Early, if you are up to it."

"You know I am."

Her heart tripped with nerves. "Excellent."

Their eyes caught, lingering looks of longing hovering between them. But when his eyes dropped to her lips, and that familiar desire swirled at the base of her belly, she drew a step away.

As greatly as she wished to continue what they'd started before, she first needed to prove what she was willing to do for him. After he'd sacrificed everything for her, she wanted to prove that a marriage to her didn't have to be any more of one.

"I will see you tomorrow morning, then," she said softly.

"I can't wait."

That night, after Jane left and Marie sat near the window, brushing out her hair as she sang a song, her smile would not leave her lips, nor would the anxious turning of her stomach cease.

Tomorrow had to be perfect. Tomorrow *would* be perfect. They would return to Dorking the day after, and there, the stresses of reality would be upon them once again.

But in the morning, Marie had one final chance to convince Charles that perhaps an annulment *wasn't* what they wanted after all.

"We're here."

Marie spoke beside Charles the next day as the carriage rolled to a stop. He peered out of the window, eying the fields and other carriages the groom stopped beside.

"Where exactly is *here*?" he asked.

"You'll see," she said with a conspiratorial smile.

Charles's intrigue and joy were paramount, not only for what surprise lay ahead, but the very fact that Marie had planned this on her own. Never in his wildest imaginings did he think she would want to do anything of the sort—leave the comfort of home, travel to a town she'd revealed she'd never been to. All of it was so...*adventurous.*

Charles exited the carriage first, then offered his hand to Marie, who accepted it with a bright expression. He wondered how long it might be before she let him in on her secret, but as they moved beyond the carriages and crowds and closer into the town, he didn't need an explanation at all, for he knew exactly what she'd brought him to.

"A festival?" he said.

"A festival," Marie repeated beside him, her hand looped around his arm as they paused to take in the sight. "To remind us of the first adventure we found in common. And, perhaps, the first *real* adventure we share in together today."

Charles shook his head in disbelief. All of this was unthinkable in the best possible way. Did that mean she wished to keep adventuring with him? Did that mean she wished to stay married?

With joy threatening to topple from his heart, he cast his eyes around them.

The town was full to bursting with booths set up at various locations, tables overflowing with cakes and biscuits and cheese. A juggler tossed colorful balls into the air as he moved down the street, and children laughed at the puppet shows popped up near shops with their doors propped open.

A group of musicians played in the town square where impromptu dancing now took place between a number of couples, and makeshift fences barred in cows, sheep, and pigs. Any smell that might have exuded from the livestock was removed promptly due to a gentle breeze that pulled the scent of strawberries and brown sugar around the space.

Excitement flapped its anxious wings within Charles's chest. Never had he experienced such a thoughtful gift—for that was precisely what this was, a gift from his incomparable wife.

"You are pleased?" Marie asked, looking so adorably hesitant, he wanted to wrap her in his arms and kiss her until she knew how greatly he *was* pleased.

Instead, he pulled her hand up and soundly kissed the back of it, knowing anything further would elicit more than a few stares. "I have never been more happy, m—Marie."

Their eyes caught. He'd been about to call her, *"My darling."* He didn't wish to startle her with his sudden shift in affection toward her, and yet, as her eyes found his, warmth encompassing every inch of those chocolate depths, he wondered if she might have welcomed the words, after all.

From that point forward, Charles tested his theory as they enjoyed the sights of the fire blowers, the smells of the fresh bread and cherry tarts, and the sounds of laughter and conversation around them. He was attentive and complimentary, placing his hand at the small of her back time and time again and leading her forward with eager fingers through crowds.

He could hardly comprehend what was occurring as he walked about the space with his wife. He'd experienced far more adventurous moments—storms at sea, peering over the edge of enormous cliffs, walking through caves—but never had he enjoyed himself so fully as walking about the town with Marie on his arm, his fingers securely over her hands.

He'd always had great fun with his friends, but there had always been something missing—a companionship, a careful feminine touch—and now that he had it with Marie, he knew he would never settle for anything less.

After sampling cheeses and cold slices of meat, they wandered toward a man at the edge of town who was sending his trained falcon into flight to the amazement of the gathered crowd.

"I've always enjoyed watching birds," Charles mused aloud as the fowl returned to its master.

"They are quite fascinating," Marie agreed. "My dear friend Mrs. Chumley has just married an avid bird observer. I hear he has been attempting to put on an expedition of sorts through England."

"Now that would be an adventure in its own right," Charles said, and Marie hummed in response.

Next, they moved on to listen to the music, a group of female singers having replaced the musicians from before.

"You ought to perform," Charles said.

"Oh, no. I do not make it a habit to sing before others."

Charles had been about to claim otherwise, but he held his tongue. He wasn't quite ready for her to know that he'd been falling asleep to her beautiful singing for a week now.

After listening to the performance, they kept up their meandering past shops and booths, munching on hot pies and fresh strawberries until the sun drew close to the horizon, and the day wore out.

As the rest of the town dispersed, Charles and Marie reluctantly returned to their carriage and climbed in with sore feet and full hearts.

Once settled within the coach's walls, Charles peered at the empty seat beside her. "Do you mind?"

She gave a little shake of her head, scooting just a degree to her left as Charles settled at her right. Roses—the scent of her hair, perhaps?—plumed around him, and heat blossomed through his core as their arms pressed up against each other.

The carriage bumped down the road, and soon, Marie fell asleep, her head bobbing up and down until Charles gently coaxed her to rest on his shoulder. She sighed, settling deeper against him as heat pooled in his chest.

Charles was overcome with exhaustion, as well, but he had no desire to end the day. Tomorrow would bring Grendale, his parents, and the Oakleys, and he was not quite ready to face any of them. He enjoyed Marie's company too greatly to have to share her with anyone.

More than that, he couldn't help but fear that he and Marie might fall into who they were before. He, a juvenile individual, and she, a woman who could not be herself. Would their delicate marriage stumble upon such rocky ground?

These concerns and more continued to billow around him until his exhaustion finally overcame him, and his eyes drooped to a close.

Charles didn't know how long they'd been asleep for when a loud clunk and a jostle launched him against the carriage wall, bringing Marie to fall right into the side of him.

She yelped, and he reached out, holding her securely to keep her uninjured as the carriage tilted to its side.

Chapter Twenty-One

"What the devil!" Charles exclaimed as the horses whinnied outside and men began to shout.

The carriage stilled, tipped back on one side so he and Marie were pressed firmly against the side wall and back seat.

"What happened?" she asked, her voice filled with fright in the darkness.

Charles looked out the window, but all was black. "The carriage must have thrown a wheel."

Sure enough, a moment later, the footman came in with a harried expression. "Forgive me, Mr. and Mrs. Shepherd. The carriage lost a wheel."

"Any chance of fixing it tonight?" Charles asked, attempting to lean forward.

"Mr. Lloyd is looking into it, sir."

But the groom could not fix the damage with the darkness so thick, nor could he when Charles and the footman came to help.

Sorting through the options, Charles returned to Marie, who he'd encouraged to remain inside the carriage. "We cannot stay here in the darkness and cold all night, so we have two choices. We can continue attempting to fix the wheel—though there isn't much hope as none of us are particularly versed in carriage mending. Or we unhitch the horses, and the four of us walk back a mile to where we passed a small inn not long ago."

Marie's brows knit together. "What do you prefer?"

"I believe our best option is the inn. We'll be dry and warm there. Tomorrow morning we can look into finding the nearest stagecoach."

"Very well," she agreed.

"I should warn you, though. The inn...might not be what you are used to."

Charles, himself, had stayed in many uncleanly living quarters on his journeys around the country and throughout Europe. He was fine with such despondent circumstances, but to subject a lady to such—to subject his *wife* to such—was not something he wished to do.

Marie looked concerned for a brief moment, then brushed it aside with a smile. "Our next adventure, I suppose."

Charles had never been more attracted to her.

He took her hand, and together they walked through the darkness toward the inn, the groom and footman leading the two horses behind.

Upon arrival at the Blind Goose, the groom and footman found a place for the horses in the stables at the back, then took seats with a pint each.

Charles, however, had hoped to give Marie some rest. Of course, no such rest was had as the barman told them the only room available was shared with only one bed remaining.

He chewed on his lower lip. He wouldn't allow Marie to be alone in a shared room with who-knew-what sort of men—nor would he wish her to sleep upright all night with drunken men down here. So what was he to do?

His nerves were settled when she reached forward and placed a comforting hand on his arm, addressing the barman first. "We'll take the bed, thank you."

Charles's gaze whipped toward her.

"We *are* married, Charles," she whispered. "We shan't cause a scandal if we share a bed."

A scandal was the least of his concerns. Sharing a bed, however...

They reached the room a few moments later, four beds lined up in a row. The first three were occupied, large lumps under dark blankets, so they made their way to the final one, tucked beneath a window with a large crack in it that allowed a heavy draft to blow about the room.

"Now we know why there was one left," Charles muttered under his breath.

A snorting occurred in the bed next to them, and a lump tossed back and forth before settling again. Marie watched them warily, as well.

"I'm sorry about this," Charles whispered.

She merely shrugged. "You warned me. At any rate, now when you speak of your ship tossed about at sea, I shall be able to speak of a night spent at a potentially duplicitous inn beneath a broken window next to three snoring, adult men."

Charles couldn't help but grin.

"And," she continued, "at least we do not have to deal with any great stench hulled up in that corner."

"Right you are."

And yet, when they faced their sleeping arrangements, he still hesitated. Compared to the inn's mattress, Woewood's beds had seemed fit for a king. This one was hardly large enough for the both of them—and there was no chance they would be able to share it without touching.

"I'll sleep on the floor beside you," he offered in a whisper.

"You most certainly will not. It's covered in mud."

He eyed the smears of muddy footprints strewn about the floor, visible from the light of the moon pouring in from the window. "But the bed isn't large enough for the both of us."

"As I said before, we *are* married."

"But our arrangement..."

"The annulment?" she clarified.

He couldn't care a lick about the annulment any longer. He merely wished for Marie to have the option, should she still wish for it.

Please, do not let her wish for it.

"Yes, the annulment," he replied.

"As if we are in danger of risking that here, surrounded by all of these men. Now stop your protesting and share a bed with your wife."

Her eyes twinkled, and his heart skipped a beat.

She removed her gloves, bonnet, and boots, setting them at the end of the bed on the floor before climbing onto the lumpy mattress first, fully dressed as she scooted up against the wall. She paused, eying the grey pillow with a slight wrinkling of her nose, then tried to hide her hesitance with another smile.

"Here," Charles said at once, removing his jacket and placing it face down on the pillow so she might sleep on the inside of it.

Relief filled her expression instantly. "You don't have to do that," she protested, but he insisted.

She laid down on her side, then patted the spot next to her.

Charles didn't move an inch. For the last few nights, he'd longed to lay down beside her, to hold her, caress her soft skin, but the wall between them—though paper-thin—had provided a strong enough barrier.

How was he to manage tonight?

"What's the matter?" she asked. "Do you need more room?"

He shook his head. "I do not think this is wise."

"I promise to keep my hands to myself," she teased.

"That's hardly what I'm concerned about."

"Then *what* are you concerned about?"

"That *I* won't..." he began.

She didn't respond, seeming to catch his words in an instant. "Charles, are you—"

"Quiet down over there!"

Marie jumped at the man shouting from the corner.

Charles scowled at him, though he knew he wouldn't be able to see it. He had a mind to tell the man off for shouting at a lady, but when he caught Marie's smile, he stopped.

"You'd better get in this bed now before we are kicked out of the room altogether," she said in a voice barely audible.

Charles sighed, knowing she was right. He didn't want to subject her to a night of sitting in an upright chair downstairs, so he set aside his reservations and climbed into the bed.

He first tried lying on his back, but his shoulder hung halfway off the frame, so he shifted to his side away from Marie. The bed, however, had no support in the center, so he naturally sunk toward her.

With a heavy sigh, he resigned himself to his other side facing her, holding himself away with a hand between them that rested on the inner lining of his jacket. Her hand also relaxed between them, a mere inch from his.

"Comfortable?" she asked, clearly amused with his movements.

"Indubitably."

She stifled a laugh.

"You?" he asked.

"I've been better."

He eyed her hand next to his, her long, slender fingers against his jacket. A lady as lovely as this ought not be subjected to such sleeping arrangements—in the inn or with the man who'd promised to give her an annulment if she wished for it. How could he ever live with himself if he made it so the annulment was *not* possible, if he trapped her within a marriage she didn't want?

He winced. "I'm s—"

His words were cut off by her finger against his lips. "If you attempt to apologize one more time for any of this, I shan't forgive you."

Their eyes met. He didn't say a word. Her eyes focused on his mouth until she gently slid her finger away, caressing his bottom lip in the motion.

His breathing shallowed.

Think of something else. Anything else besides those lips so close to your own. Think of the three men in the room with you. Of seeing your mother tomorrow. Of Marie wanting an annulment.

Please, Heaven, do not let her want the annulment.

"How did you know I was going to apologize?" he asked, their voices far softer now.

"You have this look in your eye," she explained. "Regret, I believe. It came when I mentioned that I overheard your conversation with your parents, and that day at the church."

Charles had no idea he was so expressive. "Well, at the risk of offending you, I *am* sorry. A lady like you ought not be subjected to sleeping like this."

"I thought you said I needed adventure?"

"I'm far too opinionated. Surely you know that."

"That is the first thing I learned about you." Her eyes swept across his features. "And that you do not hesitate to take charge when something is wrong. That is why you need not apologize. With you, I do not have to worry if a carriage wheel falls off. Just as I do not have to worry about sharing this bed with you now." Her eyes softened. "Because you are as honorable a man as they come, Charles."

If she could only read his thoughts—how desperately he wanted to pull her toward him, to place his lips to hers in a kiss that ended with both of them agreeing to remain wedded. That was his greatest desire, and there was no point denying it any longer. How he cursed the fact that he ever presented the option of an annulment to her.

"Do you know what I used to call you?" she whispered dreamily, her eyelids heavy as she blinked, as if she were half asleep already.

"What is that?"

"Childish Charlie," she whispered. "Though it was only ever in my thoughts."

Charles didn't know whether to laugh or grimace, for he'd

definitely earned the title. "That is not the most flattering name I've received," he replied. "I was hoping for something more along the lines of *Handsome Charles* or *Charming Charlie*."

She smiled, her eyes on his mouth. Her hand raised, hesitating a moment before sliding the tip of her finger along his bottom lip once again. "Now, I am more apt to call you *My* Charlie."

His heart rapped against his chest, desperate to break free and join Marie, but he held it back.

He would not lose his control around the woman, no matter his heart's desire.

He loved her too much to risk it now.

Chapter Twenty-Two

M arie didn't want to encourage Charles any more than she already was, for her desire to be near him was so strong, she was hardly thinking straight, her mind teetering between conscious and dreamlike states.

The day had been perfect, and now, ending it in Charles's bed? She couldn't have planned it better herself.

Although, *had* she planned it, there certainly would not have been three other men in the room with them.

She continued tracing the outline of his lips with her fingertip, her eyes growing heavy.

"Thank you for today," Charles said, giving her a momentary volley of energy.

She lowered her hand on the bed next to his, their little fingers pressed together.

"I hope you enjoyed it," she replied.

"I did. More than any other adventure I have ever had."

Obviously he exaggerated, but she smiled all the same.

"Are you ready to return tomorrow?" he asked next.

Her spirits fell. She'd managed to set aside the thought of returning to Grendale Manor all day. "I suppose. I assume you are not, seeing as how we have another ball to attend."

He grimaced. "No."

"We could always make it better for you," she offered, her eyes heavy once again.

"How so?"

"You could push me into a fountain again."

He smiled, though it faded swiftly away. "In truth, I dread being around others more than attending another ball."

"I dread that, too," she whispered.

A look of understanding passed between them. Had Charles changed his mind about the annulment? The look in his eyes certainly suggested so.

A cold draught sailed through the window, pulling a lock of hair across her brow, so she nuzzled further into Charles's jacket, his earthy cologne filling her nose. Would the scent linger on her until morning? Would she be fortunate enough to smell it again if he kissed her now?

"Are you cold?" Charles asked.

"A little."

He reached forward, brushing her hair from her brow before eying her hands. "May I?"

She nodded, though she had no notion as to what he intended to do.

He pulled her hands between his in slow movements, drawing her fingers toward his lips as he blew warm, comforting breaths upon her skin.

She closed her eyes, the warmth filling her body as if the sun shone down upon her—for that was what Charles was to her. Warmth, goodness, joy. The reason her future was secured, and the reason she now wished to live.

"I am going to have trouble sleeping tonight," he whispered, breaking through another dreamlike state.

"Uncomfortable?" she murmured.

He shook his head. "I cannot seem to sleep now without your singing."

Her eyes flew open.

"The walls are thin," he explained.

Marie knew this already. She'd heard his every footstep, his every movement in bed. And yet, she'd never heard him or his valet speak a word. She'd thought that meant he couldn't hear her either.

Her cheeks warmed. "I'm not the best singer."

"On the contrary," Charles said. "You've the loveliest voice I've heard in all my years."

Once again, she knew he exaggerated, but his compliment soothed whatever embarrassment remained.

"If I wasn't afraid of you being shouted at again, I'd suggest you sing me to sleep right here."

"Perhaps another night, then," she suggested.

His eyes caught hers. "Yes. Perhaps another night."

Her heart thrummed against her chest.

"How are your hands?"

"Much warmer, thank you."

Still, he kept hold of them. "I will let you sleep now," he whispered.

Marie nodded, though that was not what she wanted at all. She wanted to be kept awake all night by Charles. Listening to his kind words, receiving his kisses, feeling his hands on hers.

But as his callused fingers gently caressed her skin, sleep crept upon her once again, and this time, Marie allowed it to take her.

The following morning, after a sleepless night, Charles and Marie caught the stagecoach and made it back to Orpington after many long, cramped hours, only to be whisked away into another carriage to return to Dorking that night for the ball. With no extra coach for the help, Marie's lady's maid and Charles's valet accompanied them, allowing no chance for the private conversation Charles so desperately wished to have with his wife.

Last night had settled any remaining concerns he had about

their relationship, for he knew his feelings for her had changed. All he needed to do was be sure hers had, as well. Based on her actions the day before, he was more hopeful than ever, but he had to be sure.

All he needed to do was catch her alone. All he needed was Marie. *Only* Marie.

And yet, his hopes were dashed away again when they reached Grendale, for no sooner did the carriage stop before the front doors did his mother and father pour out to greet them with anticipatory smiles and hopeful eyes.

Charles remained mostly silent, but Marie was as generous as ever, vaguely answering their questions about their time away before gently directing the focus to the upcoming ball.

"Yes, we haven't much time to speak, do we?" Mother said somewhat disappointedly. "People shall begin arriving shortly, no doubt. Perhaps we may speak later...about your time at the cottage?"

Marie promised to do so, glancing at Charles as a subtle hint to respond, as well.

"Yes, of course," he mumbled.

He couldn't care less about telling his mother what had occurred. All he wanted to do was speak with Marie. But when Mother pulled her away, agreeing that they must make ready for the ball, Charles was left disappointed again.

He raced through getting ready with the valet, being tempted at least half a dozen times to walk through their adjoining door, take her in his arms, and give her the proposal she deserved—a proposal that declared just how much he loved her and just how much he prayed she would spend the rest of her life with him.

But he could hardly do so if she were in a state of undress or if her lady's maid was present. He wished for his declaration to be memorable. Loving. And most importantly, private.

So instead of barging in on her, he waited, pacing back and forth about his room, ignoring piles of business letters needing attention on his desk and wishing he were back in the cottage so he could hear if she was finished or not.

Just before the last of his patience drained, Charles headed for the adjoining door. Let propriety be hanged. He needed to declare his love.

He raised his hand to knock, but another tapping sounded behind him. His heart skipped a beat. Had Marie used the other door?

With quick feet, Charles answered the knocking, his disappointment keen as his valet appeared instead.

"Yes?" Charles asked gruffly.

"Forgive the intrusion, sir, but Mr. Page has arrived from London and requests an audience in the library."

Dread pulled its heavy weight across Charles's shoulders. Weeks ago, he would have died for news from his steward. Now, he cursed the man's timing. Charles couldn't put off speaking with him, either. Not when Marie deserved to know what the steward had determined.

What *had* Mr. Page determined?

Charles's stomach churned. He peered over his shoulder, staring at their adjoining door before squaring his shoulders and leaving his room. In a matter of moments, he stood with Mr. Page, holding his breath as he listened to the steward's knowledge.

"I've good and bad news, sir," Mr. Page said. "I've discovered that one has the grounds to request an annulment if there is evidence that both parties were forced to sign the wedding document, which I believe both of you have." He hesitated. "The bad news, however, is that no matter how hard I searched for an answer, there is absolutely no guarantee that an annulment would not injure either you or your wife's reputation."

Charles took the news in stride. This was exactly the answer his logic had expected. And yet, no relief came. He may no longer feel trapped within his marriage, but Marie *might*.

The last fortnight flashed through his mind. The looks she'd given him, the way she'd kissed him, how she'd brought him to the fair for their first adventure together. Then Tristan's voice rose within his mind.

"You're a fool, Charles."

Hope took flight in his chest. He *was* a fool. And often. But tonight he wouldn't be.

———

Marie had seen Mr. Page arrive.

"The guests are already here?" Jane had asked.

But when they'd both peered down from the window, they'd recognized the steward instead.

Marie hadn't been able to concentrate since, and the moment Jane left her room, Marie's eyes flicked to Charles's door.

Was he in there waiting to share the news with her? Or would he wait for tomorrow?

Well, Charles may want to wait, but she could not. Picking up her soft pink skirts and heading toward the adjoining door, Marie forced herself to take courage. She had no hope of spending another ball in front of a crowd pretending that all was well between her and her husband—when she did not *know* if all was well. Things could have changed for Charles. Being around his parents again could have reminded him of his feelings from before —how trapped he was within this choiceless marriage.

She hesitated a moment before softly knocking on the door, but no answer came. Twice more she knocked, and twice more there was no reply.

Was he speaking with Mr. Page downstairs, or had he perhaps fallen asleep from their rigorous journey?

Slowly, she opened the door a crack with another knock. "Charles?"

No response came. She entered the room more fully, greeted at once by the smell of his cologne and the tidy nature of the space —aside from the mess of letters strewn about his desk.

Still, there was no sign of Charles.

With a sigh, she made to retreat. As she turned, she brushed too closely against the desk, and a few letters fluttered to the floor.

Swiftly, she picked them up and stacked them together before laying them on the desk. She made to turn away, but when her eye snagged on her own name written upon the top correspondence, she froze.

This is not yours, Marie, do not read it.

But her eyes were faster than her conscience as her gaze swept down the paper.

I am sorry to say this, Mother, but I cannot do this any longer. My marriage to Marie is a farce. I should like to be clear and honest with you by letting you know that we are seeking an annulment. She and I have nothing in common, and this is the only way for us to find true happiness—by being apart.

The words blurred together as Marie's eyes filled with tears. This couldn't be. She had to have imagined what she'd read. Charles had to be speaking of something else.

And yet, her name in his writing was clear—as clear as his desire to still end their marriage.

But how could that be so? What of the moments they shared, the way he'd looked at her in bed only last night? The kind words he'd spoken and the connection they'd made? She couldn't have imagined it all.

And yet, as she read Charles's words again, her cheeks flamed. How foolish she'd been to have had even the smallest hope that Charles would remain with her by choice. Of course he would choose his freedom. What person wouldn't?

Drying her eyes, she steeled herself against any remaining emotion. There would be no place for the shedding of tears this evening. She had to attend the ball and keep up appearances one final time.

Tonight, she would be Immovable Marie Oakley again...instead of brokenhearted Marie Shepherd.

Chapter Twenty-Three

The entryway filled swiftly with guests as Charles and his parents welcomed the attendees of the ball. Though he spoke with each individual who passed him by, his attention was fixed to the top of the stairs.

Marie had yet to make her appearance, and her tardiness was beginning to worry Charles. Had something happened to prevent her from joining them earlier? Was she in need of his service of some sort?

Just before he could convince himself to check on her, she appeared at the top of the stairs, and the breath was snatched from Charles's lungs.

Marie's pink skirts fluttered about her legs as she walked down each step, the color of the gown matching the shade of her cheeks. Her dark hair was sprinkled with pearls, and her graceful, gloved hand trailed down the banister with gentility.

She was stunning. But then, Marie was always stunning.

"Are you ever going to tell me how your time at the cottage went?" Mother asked beside him, staring up at Marie, as well.

"After tonight, I won't have to," he said enigmatically.

Mother's eyes shone with delight. "Oh, Charles. I cannot

express how delighted I am to hear that. Especially after...after I..." She trailed off. "I am so sorry for how all of this came about."

Charles smiled, despite himself. Her apology was welcome and accepted, but he realized he didn't need it any longer. "You aren't sorry, Mother."

She pulled back.

"How can you be," he began, "when it ended precisely how you wished it to?"

She fought off a smile for as long as possible before patting his cheek with affection.

More guests arrived, but Charles slipped away from the welcoming line, making directly for Marie.

Her eyes had yet to meet his as she reached the bottom step, but when he stood before her, their gazes finally met.

Instantly, he frowned.

"Are you well?" he asked, noting the red in her eyes that hinted at past tears.

"Yes," she said, pulling on a static smile. "You are looking very fine this evening, Mr. Shepherd."

Charles wasn't buying the act for a moment. "What is it?"

She glanced around them, as if keenly aware of the eyes upon them. "Nothing. I am merely tired from all of our traveling today." She nodded at a passerby. "I understand Mr. Page arrived just before the ball."

Charles hesitated. He had no intention of declaring his love for the woman right there in the center of Grendale's entryway, nor did he wish to be rejected in the same location.

But Marie had the right to know the truth about their annulment as much as she had the right to know of his feelings for her.

"He did," he finally replied.

She looked away. "Excellent. I should like to hear what he had to say so we may move forward with the annulment."

His heart pinched. Before he could say anything in response, she was off, standing at Mother's side and greeting one of their neighbors.

Charles stared after her, eying her graceful movements and that smile that didn't reach her eyes. He couldn't believe she truly wished for the annulment. He *wouldn't* believe it.

The guests arrived in full-force, then, and Charles did his duty by greeting each one, introducing those who had not yet met Marie. This time, he accepted words of congratulations with sincerity, though Marie's distanced behavior continued.

When all were in attendance and the first song announced, he made to ask her to dance, but she was already occupied for the first set. Desperate to not recreate their first ball together, Charles pulled his mother to dance in the same set as Marie so when the song ended, he had a direct line to his wife.

With a smile and an offered hand, he reached her. "May I have the next dance?"

She hesitated. "Is that wise?"

He supposed it was customary for married couples to ensure single individuals had partners, but when had he ever been one to do as Society suggested?

"I believe we will be forgiven just this once," he said.

Marie averted her gaze, though she took his offered hand all the same as he led them toward the floor.

Facing her, he tried to catch her eye. "Have you had a nice evening thus far?"

"Very pleasant."

Worry stirred within him. This distance she was creating between them, this strained conversation returning, was far too reminiscent of how they'd begun their marriage. This was what he'd feared—Marie reverting to who she had been, a woman who could not be herself.

But he was a different man now, and he would not go down without a fight.

The music began, and Charles reached for her hands. She missed a beat, scrambling to catch up, but he adeptly helped her correct her mistake.

More steps were taken as they circled around each other, and all the while, Marie kept her eyes anywhere but on Charles. He soon discovered why, however, as he caught her swiftly swiping at a tear that glimmered down her cheek.

His heart slipped. She was crying. This was not how he'd wanted their first dance to turn out. This was not how he'd wanted any of it to turn out.

"Marie," he whispered as they waited for the top couple to dance down the line. "Please, speak with me. What is the matter?"

She cleared her throat. "I..." She shook her head, then backed away from the set altogether. "I'm sorry. I cannot do this."

With a final shake of her head, she turned on her slippers and fled.

Startled glances from those around the set shifted between her and Charles, but he hardly noticed.

"Marie," he called out, walking directly through the set as he charged forth in her direction.

But she was too quick, slipping around the crowds until she vanished from his sight.

He paused near the refreshment table, looking left and right as panic flapped in his chest. He had no notion as to why she cried, but he knew he had put this off for too long. He couldn't let the night go by—another *minute* go by—without telling her the truth.

"Charles?"

He whirled around, Mother coming up to him with a worried brow and Mr. Oakley right on her heel, his expression far less forgiving.

"What in heaven's name is going on?" Mother continued. "We just saw Marie—"

"You saw her?" Charles interrupted. "Where did she go?"

Mr. Oakley scowled. "What have you done to upset her? She was crying, and my daughter never cries."

Before, Charles had very little time for the man. Now, he could not even stomach seeing him. "This is none of your concern, sir."

"She is my daughter," he barked out. "I have every right—"

"She is my *wife*," Charles interjected firmly.

Mr. Oakley stopped, his nostrils flaring.

Charles had an entire speech lined up for the man—words about how greatly Mr. Oakley had damaged his daughter and how he'd had no right to send such a disparaging and assuming letter to her—but time was of the essence. Marie was more important than a lecture right now.

Charles gave Mr. Oakley one more stern look, then faced his mother. "Please, where did she go?"

With wide eyes, she replied. "On the balcony, son."

He made to leave, then paused, resting a comforting hand on Mother's arm. "I promise I will tell you everything later. But for now, you must trust me."

Mother nodded in an instant, obviously unused to seeing Charles in such a serious state, but he didn't have time to explain.

He fled from the ballroom, side-stepping couples with their drinks and dodging pursuant older women until he reached the balcony. From there, he peered out into the darkness, pleading with Heaven before catching sight of a flash of pink disappearing down the steps.

He didn't miss a beat, taking the stairs two at a time and ignoring the startled looks of other couples who had slipped out to enjoy the night air on the balcony.

When he reached the base of it, he spotted her tucked away in the darkness, leaning against the side of the house.

"Marie?" he asked softly.

She started. "Charles? What are you..."

He slowed his steps, taking in the sight of her tear-streaked cheeks glinting in the moonlight above them. The soft murmur of the ballroom sounded above, but no other guests had made it off the balcony, leaving the two of them *finally* alone.

"You shouldn't be out here with me," she said with a shake of her head. "It will ruin our chance for an annulment if rumors sprout."

"I do not care."

"How can you say that?"

"Because it is true." He closed the distance between them, ready to be finished with the secrets and the hidden feelings. He was ready for the truth. "Why did you run from me? Did you not wish to dance?"

"No, I didn't."

"Why?"

"Because," she began, then ended with a sigh. Her shoulders slumped forward, and she leaned against the wall behind her. "Because I could not see the purpose in doing so if you are not to remain my husband."

A soothing warmth spread from his chest, and this time, he didn't stamp it out.

"That is what you heard from Mr. Page, is it not?" she continued, her hand uselessly flapping down at her side.

"He did speak with me, yes," Charles said softly. "He told me that since we were both forced into this marriage, an annulment could be sought after. But there is no guarantee that our names would remain untarnished. Especially after the time we've spent together—alone— in the cottage."

She wiped away another tear, her gloves already removed and clasped in her left hand. "You needn't worry on my account. I am perfectly capable of handling Society's rejection."

"Is that what you want? Do you still wish to end our marriage?"

She stared up at him, a vulnerability crossing her features before she pushed herself away from the wall and raised her chin. "I do not wish to be with a man who does not wish to be with me."

Charles drew a steadying breath. "What of being with a man who does?"

Chapter Twenty-Four

Charles held his breath, awaiting an answer.

"I saw your letter, Charles."

He paused. That was not the response he'd expected. "What...what letter?"

Marie hung her head. "The one you wrote to your mother."

"I did not write a letter to my mother."

She eyed him with a dubious look. "There is no use pretending. I saw it this evening on your desk. I know I shouldn't have looked, but I caught my name and read your words—how you would be happier without me and how we are still pursuing an annulment. The only reason you have chased me down now is to ease your own conscience. It has nothing to do with your own desires."

Charles's mind raced. A letter to his mother. On his desk. A *letter*...

Realization dawned. He breathed out a breath of relief, taking another step toward her. "No, Marie. No."

She stared up at him, her eyes still flooded with tears, so he reached forward, taking her hands in his. "That letter was written long ago, upon my arrival at the cottage. It must have been shuffled together with my other letters of business I have yet to sort through."

"What?" she breathed.

"I wrote that letter when I was still frustrated." He smiled softly. "You know, Childish Charlie?"

He could see her mind working to make sense of matters. "You weren't saving it for any reason?"

"No, not at all. I had forgotten of its entire existence until just now."

She looked away. "But then, why did you wish to speak with me tonight if not to tell me that Mr. Page has provided us with a way out of our marriage?"

Charles sobered. "Because it was my duty to tell you. I am sorry if you wish for the annulment still, for his news confirms that it would not be wise to do so for either one of us. I will abide by whatever decision you make." His heart raced. "However, please allow me to tell you my own opinion on the matter first."

Marie could hardly breathe. "What is your opinion, Charles?"

He stared down at her, his eyes caressing every inch of her features. "My desire is to remain married to you forevermore, Marie."

Emotion stuttered her heart. "You truly mean that?"

He let out a chuckle, running his hands through his hair. "I cannot tell you how *truly* I do mean it. I have lived every day in agony since suggesting the annulment. Each time a letter did not arrive, I was filled with relief, and each time you brought it up, my hopes were dashed away once again. I cannot imagine anything worse than ending our marriage before it has even begun, Marie. I have fallen for you. I never thought it possible to love someone as much as I love you, and in so short amount of time, but it is true."

He stopped, his swift speech causing his chest to rise and fall with heavy breathing. Reaching forward, he ran the back of his fingers along her cheek, his words slowing with his movements. "You are everything I have ever wanted in a wife. Everything I have ever wanted in a companion. I cannot imagine a life without you in it—I do not *want* to imagine a life without you in it."

Marie couldn't believe she was hearing these words coming from Charles. *Her* Charles. She smiled, tears pouring freely down her cheeks now.

He wiped them away with a gentle thumb. "So now you have heard my desires," he said softly, "what are yours?"

"You know what I want, Charles."

"I believe I do, but still, I should like it spoken so I have no further concerns or doubt. Even in writing, perhaps."

She laughed. "You, Charles. I want you."

He blinked swiftly, and Marie suspected it was to hide his own tears, but she couldn't be sure, for in the next moment, he reached forward, cupping her face in his hands and gently caressing her skin with his touch.

"I have been wanting to do this since the first time you kissed me," he breathed, leaning in closer to her, his breath on her lips.

Her eyes struggled to remain open. "Then do not wait a moment longer, my love."

So he didn't.

His lips pressed against hers, softly, but with a firmness that told her he *meant* his kiss this time. She slipped her arms around his neck, pulling her body as close to him as possible, and he embraced her in return.

The love she felt from his mere touch was stronger than anything she had ever experienced, for in that moment, she knew she was finally safe.

After a moment, Charles pulled back, peering deeply into her eyes. "I do not want to go back into that ballroom, but I suppose we ought to."

Marie nodded. "Perhaps we ought to take a dip in the fountain first."

He laughed. "We could recreate the whole experience. Only

this time, we'd return to the ball instead of home. Imagine the looks we'd receive."

"There would be no chance for an annulment then," she teased.

He stared down at her, love apparent in his eyes. "There is no chance of an annulment now."

Then he kissed her again.

When they were finished—though admittedly, Marie was never finished kissing Charles—the two of them returned to the ballroom hand-in-hand with matching rosy cheeks and breathless smiles.

This time, the dance they shared was exactly what the two of them had hoped for—for it was a dance shared between two people hopelessly and undeniably in love.

Epilogue

"Have you finished, then?" Marie asked, coming up to stand behind Charles where he sat at his desk. "We've dinner tonight with Tristan, you remember. He said he has news of his own today. We shouldn't be late."

The sun was near-to-setting, an orange glow cast through the window and filling the room with a golden, peaceful ambiance.

She wrapped her arms around Charles's shoulders and leant down to rest her cheek against his. He leaned in, welcoming her embrace.

"I've finished just now," he said, signing his name at the bottom of the letter. "They'll be in for a surprise, will they not?"

"They certainly will."

More than a month had passed by since the ball—a month filled with bliss and joy and laughter—and only now Charles had chosen to write to his friends, alerting them of his recent marriage and of his plans to host a special house party for them all to attend so the seven of them might come together to meet his new wife.

"Do you think they will come?" Marie asked.

"I know Tristan will," Charles said, standing from his seat.

He wrapped his arms around her, and Marie responded in the same manner.

"I imagine they'll all make an effort, though," he continued. "I'm certain they will wish to see who else has any plans to wed."

"You must be relieved you don't have to pay the wager. You're welcome for that, by the way."

He placed a kiss to her brow, then her temple, then her cheek. "I do appreciate your efforts in that regard, but I must say, I'm more relieved to have my wife want to stay married to me."

She smiled as he continued trailing kisses across her features, brushing her lips in the process.

"As if I had any other choice," she said, swiftly losing focus. "The moment Childish Charlie vanished, I was lost."

He pulled up with an unimpressed look. "I thought we agreed not to use that name?"

"*You* did. I agreed to nothing of the sort."

He grimaced. "Then might I request you do not speak it in front of my friends? Particularly my brother?"

"Afraid they'll take to using it, too?"

"I'm afraid they'll see the *truth* in it," he stated.

She laughed. "I hope you know, I don't truly see you as a child."

"Even though you *are* older than me?"

She tipped her head to the side. "Does that bother you?"

"Not even the smallest amount." He pulled her in closer, smoothing his thumbs up and down her back as he held her. "In fact, I rather like it. It will certainly prove to give me a different reputation with my friends. They think me rather immature, if you can believe it, so when they discover that I not only managed to capture the most beautiful of wives, but the most mature, the most regal, and the most lovely of all women—*two* years my senior —they will be beside themselves with shock." He leaned closer to her. "In fact, they might very well be jealous that I managed to catch the eye of an older woman."

"Is that all you care about?" she teased, her mind swirling at his loving words.

"Certainly not. But after the amount of jealousy I felt when other men interacted with you, it would be satisfying to be on the other side of it."

She laughed again, then stood on the tips of her toes to finally press their lips together.

He returned it with a deep, lingering kiss, but when he scooped her up in his arms, she broke off with a joyful yelp. "What are you doing, you scoundrel?"

"Spending some time with my wife," he said with a flash of his eyebrows.

He leaned forward to kiss her again, but she pulled back with a finger on his lips. "Oh, no, you don't. We have dinner, remember?"

"Tristan can wait."

But Marie shook her head. "You know he *cannot* wait. I wouldn't put it past him to knock on our door and tell us to get downstairs."

Charles sighed. "Very well." Gently, he lowered her to the ground as he softly muttered, "Ruin all my fun."

She laughed, giving him a swat on his arm before pulling him in for another kiss. "I promise I'll make it up to you."

"How so?"

She thought for a moment. "Perhaps when your parents leave for London next, we may remain behind and have the house all to ourselves." She looked up at him with a coy smile. "We can behave however we wish. And I might even request that you eat breakfast how you did at Woewood that first morning together."

Her eyes dropped to his covered chest, and she rested a hand to it, imagining that morning a few weeks before.

Charles grinned, once again pulling her into his arms, as if he simply could not help himself. "You are my favorite, Marie."

She beamed up at him. "I'm going to be your favorite even more when I tell you I have another surprise for you."

His eyes widened. "You're with child?"

"What?" She laughed. "Heavens, no. It's far too early for that."

He looked disappointed for a fleeting moment, then shrugged. "I suppose." He gave his head a shake, then smiled with intrigue. "So what surprise is it, then?"

"I've written to my friend, Mrs. Chumley," she began.

"The one with the bird observing husband?"

"The very one. I have only now received a letter back, telling me they are moving forward with their bird observation expedition across England. They have one of the top observers in the country, a Mr. Henry Branok, coming to teach, and...I have claimed two spots for us to attend."

His eyes brightened. "What a splendid idea for our next adventure."

"You can bring along Tristan if you prefer. Or one of your other friends. I don't have to..."

She trailed off as he shook his head.

"Surely you already know," he began, his eyes searching hers, "there is no one I would rather go on an adventure with than you, my darling."

And as she peered up into his eyes, she knew he spoke the truth.

After another kiss, he took her hand in his and left the room.

"Now, come along," he said. "You weren't wrong about Tristan. I expect he'll be on his way up here already."

"What news do you think he has for us?"

Charles shrugged. "I haven't the faintest."

"Perhaps your mother has worked her magic and found a wife for him," Marie suggested.

"It certainly wouldn't be the first time," he said with a knowing look. "Or the last."

Then with a kiss to the back of her hand, he led her down the corridor. Marie leaned into him, reveling in the comfort she felt in his mere presence and knowing no matter what adventures lay ahead, all would be well with a man like Charles Shepherd as her husband.

My Charles, indeed.

THE END

Read the next book in the series today about Charles's twin, Tristan Shepherd!

A Foolish Proposal
By Kasey Stockton

The Gentlemen's Gamble

Andrew & Sophie

A Fortunate Miscalculation by Karen Thornell

Charles & Marie

An Accidental Marriage by Deborah M. Hathaway

Tristan & Caroline

A Foolish Proposal by Kasey Stockton

Rowan & Arabella

A Novel Engagement by Anneka R. Walker

Ambrose & Susanna

A Bewildered Bachelor by Holli Jo Monroe

Leonard & Honora

An Honorable Love by Audra Wells

Author's Note

INTRODUCTION

I think this might be my shortest Author's Notes I've written to date. Look at me learning to be more concise. This book was an absolute pleasure to write. So many of my books take months and months, but this one was finished within just a couple. That's probably why it was so fun to write...

BOOK OF COMMON PRAYER

I've been wanting to write a marriage scene ever since I had to delete one from Behind the Light of Golowduyn. It slowed that story down, and I was so sad to remove it, but it made writing this one all the more fun! I was able to take the direct words from The Book of Common Prayer, including the phrasing, "Will thou have this woman to thy wedded wife?" It's always amazing to add sources from the exact time Jane Austen was alive.

CONNECTIONS

Did you connect the dots to where you've heard of Charles and Marie before? Does *Love Is for the Birds* ring any bells?? The perfect-looking couple—who were already married during the bird excursion with Henry and Lark—finally got their love story in this book. It was so enjoyable connecting them in this way, and I really loved every second of it.

NAMES

When Marie and Charles go through the meanings of their names, I had no idea what they were until I looked them up. Ironic, indeed, especially concerning Charles's name.

SIMILARITIES TO MARIE

I'm not the most adventurous of individuals, but like Marie, I have my own husband who helps me see the joy in traveling and doing things outside of my comfort zone. With his help, patience, and encouragement, I've seen so many things I never thought possible. I'm so glad I was able to write a story about a woman breaking out of her shell to really *live*.

SIMILARITIES TO CHARLES

If sarcasm was a love language, it would be mine. I tell that to my husband all the time. Of course I'm being sarcastic when I say it, but not by much. Writing Charles was really fun and *really* easy, as I'm sure you can imagine.

ANGRY KISS

I can't tell you how many angry kisses I've tried to write over the years. I'd say nearly every book I write, I try to add in an angry kiss, but I take out each one because it either doesn't make sense for the characters, or it doesn't make sense for the story.

But finally—*finally!*—I got to keep an angry kiss for this book. It was a joy to write and a joy to read over each time, mostly because my desire to have one in a book of mine has finally been satiated.

TWINS

Like angry kisses, I've always wanted to write about twins, so being able to add them to the story—as well as writing the twin to be brothers with one of my best writing friends—was the best.

Before the idea came about, Kasey Stockton and I were separately looking at the images we had for our covers. We ended up both wanting to use the same model. We tried finding different images, though we continued to return to the same guy. Kasey joked about them being twins, then one thing led to another, and we finally agreed to go with it. I'm so glad we did!

THANK YOU

As usual, thank you to each of you who read this book and these Author's Notes! I'm so grateful for those of you who support clean romance, indie authors, and my books. It's hard to be an author sometimes, but it's always made worth it when readers share what they love about my stories, so don't hesitate to leave reviews wherever you can! Even if it's just spreading the word. Anything and everything helps.

If you want to learn more about me and my writing, please join me on Instagram and Facebook, then sign up for my newsletter to never miss a new release. If your interested in purchasing signed paperbacks of my novels, visit my website at www.deborahmhathaway.com.

Thank you for reading!
Deborah

Acknowledgments

I'll start off by thanking my wonderful beta readers—Kasey Stockton, Martha Keyes, Jess Heileman, Karen Thornell, Rebekah Isert, Heidi Stott, Brooke Losee, Amy Tolman, Nancy Madsen, and Michelle Henrie. You helped make this story shine, and I can't thank you enough!

I need to give a special shoutout to Kasey Stockton for holding my virtual hand as I wrote this story. Not only did you help settle my concerns, but writing our hot twins was the best thing ever. Thank you for all your help!

Thank you to my five wonderful children! You've been so supportive and understanding as I've written all these years. Sure, you get to play video games when I'm on deadlines, and I'm pretty sure that's why you encourage me to write whenever I can, but still. You guys are the best.

Christian, you're the reason I am where I am today. I'm so glad I get to have you by my side through this adventure called "life"! I love you!

Books by Deborah M. Hathaway

A Cornish Romance (Regencies)

On the Shores of Tregalwen, a Prequel Novella

Behind the Light of Golowduyn, Book One

For the Lady of Lowena, Book Two

Near the Ruins of Penharrow, Book Three

In the Waves of Tristwick, Book Four

From the Fields of Porthlenn, Book Five

Men of the Isles (RomCom)

Winning Winnie's Hand, Book One

Driving Maisie Crazy, Book Two

Ruling out Robyn, Book Three

Multi-Author Series (Regencies)

The Cottage by Coniston

Carving for Miss Coventry

To Know Miss May

Love Is for the Birds

Multi-Author Series (RomCom)

Christmas Baggage

Multi-Author Series (Christmas Regencies)

Nine Ladies Dancing

On the Second Day of Christmas

About the Author

A romantic at heart, Deborah M. Hathaway told her first love story at seven years old. Ever since, she has set her sights on writing the books she couldn't find, wholesome clean romances filled with sweet kisses and happy endings. She now writes full-time in the genre, drawing inspiration from everyday moments with her family and from her travels around the United Kingdom. When she isn't writing, Deborah can be found home-schooling her five children, tackling DIY projects with her English husband, and dreaming of one day living on a hobby farm complete with horses—preferably in the UK.

www.ingramcontent.com/pod-product-compliance
Lightning Source LLC
Chambersburg PA
CBHW031729170626
46808CB00005B/1942